BITTERSWEET

DISCARD

HOB

AND THE

PEDDLER

"HOB'S work is putting little things right,
like folding away trampled thoughts,
mending arguments, drying up spilled tears,
unkicking bruises, or unscorching the milk pan."

HOB is a friendly house-dweller, happiest when
all his problems are small ones and a cup of tea
waits for him in the fender. On the road and
without a home, he meets a peddler, who'll "travel
until traveling is over," with a magpie named
Pyke and a donkey that thinks it's a racehorse.
Invited aboard their moving home, Hob finds out
that business is business – and he is for sale. Sold to
an ordinary family, Hob discovers an extraordinary
secret lurking in their pond, and realizes an
enormous task lies before him. Using his cunning
and resourcefulness, Hob rises to the challenge
and triumphs against impossible odds.

WILLIAM MAYNE uses language that
captures the imagination of young
readers in a unique and inventive way,
showing everyday things in a magical
new light, and making reading a joy.

William Mayne

HOB

AND THE

PEDDLER

A DK INK BOOK

For Kelda and Keira Roe
at the Punch Bowl

First American Edition, 1997
2 4 6 8 10 9 7 5 3 1

Published in the United States by
DK Ink, an imprint of DK Publishing, Inc.
95 Madison Avenue, NY, NY 10016
Visit us on the World Wide Web at http://www.dk.com

Published in Great Britain by Dorling Kindersley Limited.

A catalog record is available from the Library of Congress.

ISBN 0-7894-2462-2

Color reproduction by DOT Gradations Ltd.
Printed and bound in Great Britain
by The Bath Press.

Jacket illustration by Norman Messenger

H OB WAS STANDING in front of a cold fireplace in the dark of the midwintry night. He stood very quietly, because the big dog of the house was watching him. It had stopped dreaming a wolfish dream, and was awake, thinking wolfish thoughts.

"Hob thinks they are about Hob," Hob thought. He knew what would happen if this dog caught him. The dog did not know, because it was awake. It only knew for certain in its dreams, and dogs do not remember their dreams. But Hob can hear dreams.

"Sngrrh," said the dog, and its teeth snapped together. It was trying to imagine something.

Hob is imaginary only to people and animals who can't imagine him at all.

"This isn't the best house I have lived in," said Hob. "But if this house is right, then I'm a thing that's wrong with it, and I can't cure me."

Upstairs, children were dreaming. Hob did not like their dreadful dreams. Only the children liked their dreams. If they had nice dreams they woke up frightened. If they had nightmares they woke up happy.

"They are like that," said Hob to himself.

"What?" said the dog. Perhaps it was only a bark.

"Nothing," said Hob. It would have been better if Hob had not said nothing.

"I will get about my work," said Hob. "One day they might be glad of it." His work is putting little things right, like folding away trampled thoughts, mending arguments, drying up spilled tears, unkicking bruises, or unscorching the milk pan.

But in this house they liked it all wrong. They liked things to be left hurt and crooked and scarred. They had the big dog to frighten the world, a ferret that slept in the bedroom, and they enjoyed quarrels.

"It's the sort of thing they would invent," said Hob. "But here I am, and I must make the best of it, though that isn't what they want. I'm here until I leave, and I don't know when that will be."

Hob can't leave until certain things happen. He wondered whether the children knew how to send him away.

"They are old enough to know I am here," said Hob, with a sigh. The dog looked at that little noise, and Hob only thought the next bit. "They are old enough to know how to send me away. I wish they would."

He wished they did not know he was here, because they teased him. They poured soapy water into his sleeping place, his cutch. They pointed at him, and that hurt. They shouted at him, and that made him sad. They fed him things he could not eat.

But they had not given him what would make him leave.

Tonight they had left a wooden biscuit in the blue bowl. Hob politely took it away and hid it. They had poured him a cup of painted tea with two lumps of fur in it. Hob quietly tipped it into the sink.

On the other side of the fireplace someone had left a mince-pie full of mustard and a glass of sour milk.

"It's *that* night this very night, and those are for Santa Claus," said Hob. "But this fireplace has no chimney for him to come down."

The children had left their dirty stockings hanging close by, ready to be filled, so they must think they would be getting presents.

Hob had a naughty thought, about giving the mustardy mince-pie to the fierce dog. But that would have been unkind.

"None of this is for me," he said. "I am much older than Christmas. I remember when we only had midwinter, and things were simpler, and kinder."

He heard a noise up the stairs. There was a scamper of little footsteps, a small unkind giggle, and people jumping into bed again.

"Has someone been to my cutch?" Hob wondered. "I shall look."

His cutch is always at the top of the stairs, under the last step, where friendly mice might visit him if only the house is not full of ferrets.

Up he went, underneath the stairs, and there was his bed. Tonight something was different, someone had been there and left something.

"Have they done this for me?" he thought. "Am

I to get a present? Is Santa about to visit me?"

Because, hanging on the end of his bed, there was a red stocking, ready to be filled.

"They do care," he thought. "Those children dreaming those cruel dreams really want me to be happy. I wonder, I wonder."

Hob sat on his bed for a time, thinking that they had come to love him, that they had been worth helping, that they could be both happy and sweet.

And then something else came into his mind, suddenly. He stood up without thinking and banged his head on the ceiling of the cutch. Of course, that is the floor of the landing, and along came the ferret to see what the noise was.

Hob sat down again and stayed very still. Only his mind was turning around and around. He thought the ferret heard. It was sniffing and scratching and trying to find a way through the floor.

Hob wondered why the children could not hear it, why it did not interrupt their dreams. He expected the dog to come bounding up the stairs and do one of its dream things to him.

The ferret went away, and Hob could think his thought out.

It was a simple thought. If you give Hob clothes, then he has to put them on and leave. And here they had given him a stocking, and probably he had to put it on and leave.

But perhaps they had only hung it up for him, and it wasn't clothes.

But stockings are clothes, there's no doubt about that. "No doubt at all," said Hob. "I wouldn't be completely dressed, but one leg would be warm, and I could give the other leg a turn."

And he wanted to leave. There was nothing he could do in this house. He had been here a long time, from when the babies had been born and bitten the doctor, and cried and cried so loud that the roof had to be nailed together again. Some of the rafters were still ringing, zib, zib, zib, all the night through.

"But of course I might be going to get a better present," said Hob to himself. "The past has been hard, but the future might be good."

Then he thought it couldn't be, and it was time to see how the stocking felt. He pulled it on.

The stocking was dreadful. It was giggling with drawing pins and itches and tight places and toe-nippers and ankle-biters. Hob was in agony. He fell off his bed. He tumbled down the stairs. The ferret raged. The dog woke up. The dreaming children were riding on dragons and eating planets.

"I'm so glad," said Hob, though tears were in his eyes. "If this is what they give me I'm glad they did. I must get away. I was right to put it on."

Before anyone could notice, he was out of the house by the ferret-flap, down the path, and on the road.

"I'm not dancing," he said, in case anyone was watching. "But this stocking is too painful to walk in. All the same, I have to keep going."

At the corner he looked back. He could not go

into another house until the stocking had left him. He could not take it off himself. He could not give it away. In time it would wear out, and then he could go into another house – if he was invited, if someone said, "Come in," if someone said, "The door is open for you," if someone welcomed him.

"I wonder where I was," said Hob. The house, the children, the dog, the ferret, were all melting in his memory like a dream.

"Ferret?" said Hob. "It can't be real. It wouldn't be allowed."

Now he was on the midnight road and could see the stars all across the sky.

"Bit of a muddle up there," he thought. "Very untidy. But nothing to do with me."

He had other things to think of, like a very hurting foot.

He went on walking along the midnight road, with all the winter around him. Nothing stirred in the dark, except when the reindeer went across the sky.

"Don't bother visiting my cutch," said Hob. "I'm not there, and neither is my stocking."

He walked on, because all roads lead somewhere, and if they don't you only have to turn around and go back, since all roads come from somewhere.

Most people know where they are going before they start walking. Hob finds out when he gets there.

Hob walked along the gravel road into the day until he found a milestone to sit on.

Roads come to milestones, he remembered, and people read the news on them, all about how far it is to the next mile. "Perhaps someone will tell me that news if I wait here," he said. "Then I'll know where I am going."

Chapter Two

A T THE END of Hob's night's walk it was spring-
time. He had walked for months, not just a
night. Hob's time is like that sometimes. Now
there were lambs in fields, wound up and leaping.
There were loud yellow flowers in hedgerows. There
were quilty clouds in a blanket of wakeful blue sky.

The stocking was holding tight to Hob's right leg.
His walk had worn its sole quite away, and there were
toes looking out. "A lot of road has happened to
them," Hob thought.

Now there was nothing to do but go to sleep
all day. Hob does not want to speak to the daytime.

No daytime people look behind the milestone. Hob
knows they only read the front. He went around behind
it and made himself a sleeping place on the ground. He
put his back against the stone, leaned his pipe up beside
him, yawned like a rabbit hole, and went to sleep.

He was just woken once when something tapped
his ankle, tap, tap, tap, to wake him.

"Yes," said Hob, sleepily.

There was a worm tapping his ankle. "You're snoring,"
said the worm. "In my garden. Waking the baby. Listen."

Somewhere down in the grass the baby was yelling.

"Crying its head off," said the worm. "Hedgehog will hear and eat us all up."

Hob woke up. "I know about baby," he said. "Baby anything."

He tied a soothing Medicine Knot in the baby worm's long wormy middle. "Ah," said the baby worm, "Lovely," and went to sleep again.

Hob went back to sleep. When night came he woke up, sat on the stone, smoked his pipe, and waited.

"There'll be someone soon," he said. "Milestones at night are where night people meet."

Nothing happened. No one came to tell him anything. There was only a sparrow in a hedge to hear him, and only a hedgehog in a ditch to see him.

"No need to eat," he thought, later on, at about the time people put the kettle on. "Though it's nice to keep up old customs." He had to switch off his hungry feelings.

"Shall I get there by candlelight?" Hob asked, because he knows all the old rhymes about how far it is to Babylon. But the sparrow had gone to sleep, and the hedgehog was out for breakfast. Hob was alone in the dark.

Far down the road there was a tinkly, tiny bell noise. There was a small, slow creaking. There were tired feet trailing. A rattly something was coming along. "About as big as a wheelbarrow," said Hob. It seemed to be slower than any wheelbarrow.

"They won't be able to read the news in the dark," Hob said. "Why are they so late?"

Several things were on their way. One of them was dreaming and asleep, one of them was dreaming and awake, and another was asleep and not dreaming.

"There are dusty feet," Hob said. "There is a dusty
back, and there is a kettle, but I still can't see anything."

There was a little light, coming slowly on and on.

After a long time Hob heard wheels squeaking. He
heard someone puffing and grumbling. That was the
person who was dreaming and awake.

The person dreaming and asleep was dreaming of
waking and then thinking he was awake and staying
asleep, but longing for a cup of tea.

"That sort of dream could go on forever," said Hob.
"If that was a thinking kettle in there it would dream a
pot of tea."

The person asleep and not dreaming woke up
and chuckled very loudly. Hob thought there was
mischief there, and wondered whether to hide behind
the milestone and perhaps go to sleep again. Dreams
are one thing, good or bad, but persons that dreams
can't visit are something else again.

The little light grew steadier, and came closer.

"I shall get there by candlelight," said Hob. He
smelled hot candlefat and scorching wick. "Hello," he
called, gently, a little shout a few inches long.

The dreamer woke up. "Who's there?" he said.
"What do you want?"

"News of where I am," said Hob.

"First tell me the news of who you are," said the
woken-up person, who sat at the front of a cart with
a faded red canvas tilt. "Whoa, whoa there, wake up
and stop walking."

He was talking to the donkey pulling the cart. The donkey was not asleep, too busy dreaming about not walking any farther, ever, to stop walking.

Hob jumped off his milestone, stepped into the road, and held the bridle of the donkey. The donkey trod on the foot of Hob's stocking. Toe and heel and sole and hole were torn away.

"He's forgotten how to stop, peddler," said the third person, the one who did not dream.

Hob had met a peddler with his wagon and his donkey, traveling on his way by candlelight to buy and sell his goods at the next morning place.

The third voice belonged to a magpie. She came out of the covered part of the wagon, trimmed the wick of the candle with her beak, and ate the soot.

"Who did you say you were?" asked the peddler, raising a very tall hat indeed, with a round top and patches and darns all over it.

"Hob," said Hob. "Waiting at the milestone. Were you thinking about a cup of tea?"

The peddler thought he was. "Or was it a dream?" he said, stroking his hat and putting it on again.

"Dreams, dreams," said the magpie. "Only eggs have dreams."

"I'm stopping here," said the donkey. "Is that real grass growing there? Or another bit of dream?"

The peddler climbed down from the wagon. The magpie flew to the donkey's back and undid the harness. The donkey went to eat grass, and the magpie gathered sticks. The peddler lit a fire and hung the kettle to boil.

"I think you can see me," said Hob to the peddler. "Even when I am invisible."

"I can see you in the dark," said the peddler. "I might not be able to in daylight, but I'd know you were there."

Humans can't do that, Hob knew. Perhaps the peddler was only part human.

The magpie flew right through Hob. "Didn't see you," she said. "No one knew you were there."

"She's a fibber," said the peddler. "She's called Pyke. Now you tell me why a Hob is living in a milestone, not in a house?"

Hob could hardly remember midwinter. "People in a house gave me clothes," he said.

"People are so sloppy," said Pyke. "They couldn't have meant it."

"They didn't," said Hob. "They gave me wooden biscuits and painted tea, and clothes with pins and itches in. I thought it was a present."

"There are no presents in my trade," said the peddler. "Only buying and selling and traveling."

"And picking and stealing," said Pyke.

"But I'll give you a cup of tea," said the peddler. "If you hadn't stopped the donkey we might have gone on all night the way he dreams he's a racehorse."

They sat around the fire, the donkey munching, the magpie putting her head under her wing but still peeping out, the peddler and Hob smoking their long pipes, tea steaming in the mugs, and bread and cheese on wooden plates.

The peddler went to sleep. The magpie snored.
The donkey leaned against the milestone.

Hob wanted to mend and patch the cart. It needed
it, because it was full of little gone-wrong things. "But
I don't live here so I can't," he thought.

He watched all night. Sometimes he knew he was
awake, but people might think he was asleep. When
the night grew ragged and went away, he woke up.

The thieving magpie was beside him. "It's a pretty
thing," she was saying. "I might need a nest again one
day, you never know, and this will line it." She pecked
and pulled at Hob's leg, tugging and twisting, until she
had dragged the remaining bit of stocking from it, and
flown off to hide it.

"Oh," said Hob. "My clothes are worn out or gone.
I can live in a house again. But there is no house in
sight. And I would have to be invited."

"You are invited here," said Pyke, landing back without the stocking. "Come into our cart, under the canvas."

"We could do with company," said the peddler,
with a smile that was friendly only at the edges.
"Couldn't we, bird? We've only got each other.
Climb in, Hob, and we'll be on our way."

"Me?" said Hob.

"You," said the peddler.

Hob climbed up the little steps at the back. The
peddler lifted the steps up from the road, and there
was no way down, no way out, for Hob.

"Hob's choice is Hob's choice," he thought.
He had been invited and had to be there.

Chapter Three

HOB FOUND HIMSELF a cutch under the floor at the back of the cart, at the top of the ladder. "Might as well make myself comfortable," he said. "Even if it's not really so."

"Here we are," said Pyke. "You never know your luck."

"Or whether it is good or bad," said Hob to himself. "I think this is bad. No," he thought again. "I don't know what will happen, but the peddler and the magpie don't mind if it is bad. Hob will have to wait and see. Good is as unlikely as bad; but one of them it will be, and it's not the same for them as for me."

Rain began to rain down. The donkey began to walk, and went on walking. Hob slept in his rattly cutch, with the wet road moving slowly below, splashing up and soaking Hob's tobacco.

Late in the day the donkey got to a place where it was not raining, and stopped. When the donkey thought the day was over, that was where they stayed the night. "I've stopped being waterproof," he said, "and there's all the time in the world."

"So much time has been used up in this world,"

said the peddler, "that there isn't a lot left."

He lit a little fire and brewed a cup of tea.

All night long Hob heard unknown sounds outside. There was a scraping noise, like large lumps of sugar, little lumps, and the finest and softest grains being stirred and turned, tipped and rolled.

"Can they be cooking," wondered Hob, "in the kitchen of the night?" He could smell something spicy and full of flavor. "Like pie."

The peddler snored, the donkey snored, and the magpie snuffled in her sleep, so the cart trembled. But there was another feeling, coming up from the ground, that turned the world a little unsteady.

In the morning light Hob found out what the trouble had been. There was no pie. There was no cooking. There was the sea. Just beyond the road the sea came walking past the land.

"I don't suppose you could have anything between," thought Hob. "You get sea and you get land, next to each other. Like good luck and bad luck. But what's it for? Why is it jumping up and down?"

The smell like cooking was the smell of fish and crabs and warm weed. "They've put too much salt in it," said Hob. "I don't want a slice of that, thank you, whoever you are."

The waves, jumping up and down, made the beach shake and the road tremble. They started a long way out, ran toward the land, and rushed up the sand and rocks, waving their arms and shouting.

"If they come up here I'll have to deal with them,"

said Hob. "It would take a big hanky to mop them all up, like any other mess."

But the waves always got out of breath and rushed back out to sea again, crossly dragging rocks and shingle and bits of land with them. That was what made the sugary sounds, large, little, and small.

Hob went down to taste the sugar. But it was sand, and Hob spat it out.

While he was looking at it a quick and fast wave came up the sand behind him and licked that bit of him, splash forever.

"Something is out there pushing it up here," said Hob. "Shall I ever have to find out? What's it all for?" he wondered. "Sand castles? I have never lived in a sand castle. Who does? Interesting crabs, and the children of fish, perhaps. There would be problems with wetness."

"In any case it should be tidied away," said Hob. Then he went back to the cart.

It had started off without him, but it was where he lived, so he had to run to get there.

"There's another one of those Hob things," shouted Pyke.

"One's enough," shouted the peddler. "I can make a good bargain with one Hob, but no one wants a handful. Get on, donkey, get on."

Hob had to run and walk a long way, but at last he caught up.

"Put down the ladder," he said.

"It'll be all right," said Pyke. "He can't get aboard if he's not invited. You're not invited," she told Hob.

Hob climbed the ladder. "But here I am, you ridiculous bird," he said.

"Glad we didn't lose you," said the peddler. "A house needs a Hob, and every Hob needs a house."

Pyke chuckled and chattered. "Don't say too much," she told the peddler. "He doesn't know."

"I'm home," said Hob. "This is my house. I was invited here."

Pyke laughed again, and the donkey said, "Stop it. I can't pull that sort of noise. We thoroughbreds are nervous."

"This is my cutch," said Hob, and got into it. "They're just teasing," he said. "I hope." He went to sleep because it was daylight. He nearly had dangerous dreams because he was not sure what was happening or what anyone meant. It was very strange to be in a cutch that was not in a house.

The dreams might have been better than what happened.

The cart went away from the sea, because the donkey followed a road that went that way. "I never make things up," he said. "It takes me all my time to get there, never mind inventing it first. And I've got to talk to friends. Cousins, you know." He had been having a conversation with two plow-horses just beyond the hedge.

"He's small," said one of them. "For a horse."

"We're big," said the other. "For horses."

"Time to be moving," said the peddler, waving his hat.

In the afternoon the cart stopped in front of a farmhouse standing on a low mound of grass.

Hob woke up and looked around, and saw that this was a dull sort of dream and he could go truly back to sleep again. There was quiet countryside, a few trees around a black pond, and a cow in a field.

It was a sleepy place, a place that had not quite woken up, but might do someday.

"It doesn't want to be noticed," said Hob.

"We'll see about that," said Pyke.

The peddler went in at a white garden gate. "Wait there," he said. He went to the door of the house and was invited in.

"I'll wait anywhere," said the donkey. "Could do with a little wisp of hay from the farm, maybe." But no one listened.

"Where has the peddler gone?" asked Hob.

"To sell something," said Pyke. "That's what peddlers do, buy and sell."

"Buy and sell what?" asked Hob.

"Stuff," said Pyke, in her magpie voice. "Stuff." She laughed so much that she fell off her perch and out of the cart, giggling and croaking.

"I never did like her," said Hob. "I'll go to sleep again. I'm too busy to be awake when nothing is happening. I'll sleep through it all."

He got into his cutch and closed his eyes. "I can't wake up every time the peddler sells and buys."

After a long time the peddler came out of the house. He went to the pond, waded in up to his knees, bent over, dipped his tall hat in, and brought it out full of something too dark for Hob to see. "Especially by daylight," said Hob. "So that isn't water."

The peddler came out through the gate to the cart again, carrying the hat full of darkness that was not water in his hands.

"There is something wrong with this dream," said Hob. "Black, and dark, and that bird. What is that dark stuff?"

"Oh, good night," said the donkey, slowly looking round. "What are we up to now?"

Out through the gate came some other people, the farmer, his wife, and a boy and girl.

"Going to sell it," shrieked Pyke. "Told you so."

"What?" said Hob. "What are we going to sell?"

"A bargain is a bargain," said the peddler. "Wait and see."

He came to Hob and suddenly folded the piece of darkness around him. "Gift-wrapped," he said, tucking the darkness all around Hob.

Hob felt very dreamy and swimmy, also very wide-awake because of the cold darkness like night. He wondered what it could be.

"This will do the job, Farmer George," said the peddler. "This is what you need to help with your troubles."

He picked Hob up now. Hob looked out from darkness into light. He had no idea what was happening, only that he was awake when he meant to be asleep.

"Besides," he said out loud, "Hob does not get carried. Hob walks himself about. That's the rule."

"If he knows where he is going," said the peddler.

He said to the farmer and his wife and two children at the house, "Here he is. Take him."

"Nice work, peddler," said Pyke.

"There you go, Hob," said the peddler. He held Hob out in the bundle, and George gave the money for him and took Hob in his arms.

Chapter Four

"ARE YOU SURE it will work?" asked George. "Could it be useful? Can it help?" He jiggled Hob up and down to see how heavy he was. "I suppose there is something in here? How do I look after it? It isn't like any other livestock."

"It keeps itself," said the peddler. "One genuine Hob. Hob is a bargain. Hobs usually cost the earth, but this one fell off the back of a cart, so it's cheap at the price."

"One genuine Hob?" said Hob. "Me? You've sold me?" He had never been sold before. He wondered what it would be like. He was quite awake because of the darkness around him, awake, and cross, and not a bit dreamy.

"I must be excited," he said to himself, all muffled in the black stuff. "I don't get cross. This piece of darkness, I wonder what it is. Where did it come from?"

But by then he was being looked at by George, Sally his wife, and their children. They folded back the black stuff and thought they could see him.

Pyke was cheering in a rough and noisy way. "Glad to be rid of it," she was saying.

"You'll find the bird useful, too," said the peddler. "That's you, magpie, in the bargain with Hob."

"Me?" shouted Pyke. "You've sold me?" She kept

the rough noisiness, but stopped cheering.

"No," said the peddler. "I gave you away, bird. Stay here and keep an eye on that Hob until I come around again. The donkey and I will continue to travel until traveling is over."

"You come right in, little Hob," said Sally, setting him down on the ground on his head because she could not see him clearly. "That moth-eaten bird can live outdoors."

Hob was told to go in, so in he went, through the white gate. The peddler's bargain was happening.

Beyond the gate was a farmhouse with a thatched roof, a door that touched the ground, a real chimney, and a garden that would always be with it. Not like the landscape that kept changing around the peddler's cart. The pond was beyond the garden and the farmyard, quite black.

"Views should keep still," said Hob. "So that's an improvement."

The children led him into the house.

"These are just children," said Hob. "Careless, untidy, dirty faces, never wipe their boots, don't know what seven times seven is. But not wicked, or cruel. It'll be all right." Hob does not know about seven times seven either, and it will never matter to him, but cruel has happened.

The children were all right, but there was something about the place that Hob did not quite like, something he had never met before.

"Probably the peddler," said Hob. "Or that bird."

The children pulled away the darkness that had been tied around him and dropped it untidily on the floor, grimily smudging their faces with it, grubbily treading in it with their boots. Never thinking about seven times seven.

They weren't thinking about being friendly, only about having this new toy. But it was sad for them, because Hob is invisible unless he wants to be seen, or if he is startled. Now he stayed out of sight, and the children had to search for him.

"Don't cry," said their mother, Sally. "You don't see Hob, you just treat him nicely."

"But we want to see him," the boy said. His name was Michael.

"Then we'll know him next time," said the girl, whose name was Katie.

They went on looking, while their mother put outside all the black wrapping she could gather up.

Hob went outside again. He found a milestone beside the road. "Good," he said. "I'll know where I am. A house without a milestone is nowhere."

He heard the peddler's donkey wishing for something, but not bothering to say what it was. "Because no one ever takes any notice," he said. "Oh, it's you, Hob."

"What are you wishing for?" asked Hob.

"It's not quite a wish," said the donkey. "I gave those up because they don't happen. But I think that what I'd like best is a lovely drink of water, because there was only the sea last night, and it's too big to drink, and doesn't taste as if it has ever been washed, and it has little things in it."

"Stay here," said Hob.

"Shan't move," said the donkey. "You know how donkeys are — can't, don't, shan't, won't, haven't, didn't, wasn't, wouldn't, and forgotten how."

Hob went off to find a bucket in the farmyard. There was a hole in it, but Hob turned the hole the other way up so that water wouldn't run out of it but only in.

He went to the pond. "If the peddler can walk in, so can I," said Hob. He put the bucket down into it and filled it up.

He carried the bucket to the donkey. It was very clear water, but Hob could not see the bottom of the bucket. "I expect it's swirling around," he said, "so drink it carefully."

The donkey licked his lips and put his muzzle in to suck the water up. Then he took his face out.

"I don't know where you got this, Hob," he said, "but there's something wrong. This water is strong, and pure, and not at all muddy. But I can't drink it because it is moody. It doesn't want to be drunk. Perhaps it's too proud for donkeys and doesn't know I ought to be a racehorse."

"I'll pour it away," said Hob. "I'll find some other water for you."

The water would not pour away. It stayed in the bucket. It did not like the bucket to be tipped up at all. It stood there, not moving, as if it was heavy and stiff.

"Stubborn as a donkey," said the donkey. "I can understand that. We know our own mind."

"I'll put it back where it came from," said Hob. "That's where it wants to go."

Hob carried the water back to the pond. Now
the water allowed itself to be poured out.

"I wonder what this place is," said Hob. "This is
the strange thing I felt in the house. Ponds should
have ducks and things in them. Frogs. Bulrushes.
Insects skating about. Ripples. Old boots. But there
is just dark, still water, and then the edge, and that's it.
No tadpoles, no pretty fish. I do not know what it all
is, and I shall have to look."

He found fresh water, water in a good temper,
in the farm trough.

"That's more like it," said the donkey. "That goes
down a treat. Don't swim in that other stuff, Hob.
There's something big in it."

"I shan't put a finger in it," said Hob.

Then the peddler was at the cart, the donkey
began to walk and pull, and Hob was left behind.

"It isn't a bad bargain," he thought. "The people
are friendly. The pond isn't, that's all, but I don't need
to go there. I'm not a pond person."

He had forgotten the magpie. She came looking
for him, landed on his shoulder, held it tight with her
claws, and nipped his ear with her beak.

"Keeping an eye on you," she shrieked.

"Sorry," said Hob. "I should be invisible."

He turned himself invisible at once. But he was still
there, and Pyke felt with her beak and nipped his nose.

Hob turned himself not-there-ish. That was how he
treated rain, so that it went through him. The magpie
fell through him now, and ended up on the ground,

pecking at a stone and hurting her beak.

"It's time for you to go in," she said, sniffily, because her beak was running a bit.

Hob went into the house. There was a fire inside. There were scones, there was toast. There was tea. There was a space inside the fender.

"So dark outside," said Sally. "The day should be longer than this."

Something came into the room, sliding under the door and spreading across the floor. It was black, like soot, and it lay thin on the floor but looked deep, as if you could see into it forever.

There were bright parts to it, like sparks.

"Quite dark outside," said George.

Hob understood what the black stuff was, and why the day seemed shorter. The black stuff was what he had been wrapped in. It was a patch of night, and the bright parts were stars.

"I can deal with this," said Hob. He gathered up the piece of night and rolled it tight and black. When he was outside he threw it into the air.

It went sadly around the garden in the daylight, in black patches, looking for the rest of night. It scattered pale stars that faded to gray.

The magpie came walking past, hoping to be let in.

"Shoo," said Sally.

She pulled the door closed, with Hob inside.

"My work is in here," he said. He climbed back into the fender and let the fire warm him. "And I haven't quite finished my cup of tea."

Chapter Five

"I

T WAS HUNDREDS of years ago," Sally was saying,
in her motherly way, to Michael and Katie. Hob
was yawning in the firelight. The inside of his
mouth grew warm and forgetful. Perhaps Hob was
quite asleep some of the time.

"Hob doesn't know what's important," he decided.

"Perhaps it was a thousand years," Sally went on.
"A long time, at any rate."

"You should have written it in your diary," said
Katie. She was sitting on her mother's knee, and this
was a bedtime story.

But a true one, Sally said. "Long, long ago," she
went on, "there were ships in a big river that ran into
the sea at this very place. This house was on the edge
of the beach. Now all that's left of the river is the
pond, which was the deep part, where the ships tied
up. They say it would be so full of ships you could
walk from side to side without falling in."

There was no bridge, so the ships were the only
way across.

"The ships came from far away. They came across
the sea with barrels of wine, with bundles of silk, with
sweet-scented wood, with elephants and camels, with

ivory and boxes of gold, with colored glass and tubs of honey, with currants and spices, oranges and onions."

"Did any of it fall in the pond?" asked Michael.

"Will it be full of treasure?" asked Katie.

Hob was not understanding much of the story because nothing was happening. Hob likes stories where ordinary household people, like Hob, go and have an adventure with swords and dangers and frightening lightning, and then come home and sit in the fender and go to sleep. "That is not how life should be," he said out loud. "It is only how stories should be." His eyes closed, and he thought he would not listen anymore.

"We have never seen a ship," said Michael. "Do they come at night when we are asleep?"

"You must wake us up," said Katie.

"We have seen the sea," said Michael.

"So have I," thought Hob. "It comes up behind you and gives you a wet lick. It sucks away the sand under your feet and gallops off again."

"The sea is beyond the farm fields now," said Sally. "There are roads and hedges. They say the peddler bought the fields from the sea, but that is just a story."

"There are no ships in the pond," said Katie. "I have looked. There is only funny water."

"Perhaps it is full of pots of honey," said Michael.

Boys think of food, Hob knew.

"They say that there is a big treasure in it," said Sally. "Perhaps it is only a story. Perhaps a king lost it."

"Treasure," said Michael. "I will find it."

"It's best not to," said Hob. But no one heard.

"Something is dangerous," said Sally. "Don't look. Your father and I never have. It is too near the house. That is all."

"Something is snoring in the fender," said Katie.

That was Hob. He sat with his pipe in his hand, gazing at the fire and falling asleep.

"Not me," said Hob.

"And now it is sneezing," said Michael.

"It is Hob," said Sally. "Do not tease him or talk about him behind his back. It is good luck to have him in the house."

The children went to bed to have dreams of toffee and of sliding in the hay.

Outside the house the magpie went to sleep under the eaves. She did not dream. Her dreams hid in the house because they dared not have anything to do with a magpie. They came to talk to Hob.

"We've got to do our duty and be dreamed," they told him. They did not know of anything else to do. If they went back undreamed there would be trouble for them. They might even be broken up and used to fill storybooks. "There isn't any dream space in a magpie's head," said the dreams.

"Just don't bother me," said Hob. "Anything would be better than getting into a magpie's head."

So Katie dreamed of being in a nest with other baby birds, and Michael of flying around the trees, higher and higher.

When the last candle had been blown out Hob began to see where he would live. He usually made his cutch high underneath the stairs, between downstairs ceiling and upstairs floor.

There was upstairs floor here, but no ceiling under it. There was no cutch here.

"A good, big spiderweb would do," said Hob. "Like a hammock." But there was no spiderweb in the right place.

"Besides," said Hob, "housewives do such a lot more dusting these days, I might be swept up. Mistakes can happen. I haven't found any small spiders. But."

He said "But" because he had found something very large. At first he thought it must be a sea spider because of its size, a sort of crab much bigger than usual.

"Or," he thought, "it came from another world, on one of those ships. I'd better have a look in case it eats a child. Last time I was in a house one of those would have been useful; but Hob mustn't think like that even if he wants to."

Hob stopped thinking like that. But every now and then Hob remembers he has forgotten something without knowing what it quite was.

"Perhaps I should leave it alone," he told himself. "It isn't having any dangerous thoughts."

The spider was behind a wardrobe.

"I want to make a hammock," said Hob, "if you have some spare silk."

"I'll just get some air," said the spider. "It's all down in my nest." She scampered about under the wardrobe and came back covered in bubbles.

She was a Giant Water Spider, from a pond. She had been brought up to save all the air she could because she usually lived under the water, coming up only to breathe and take bubbles down to the nest. Now she was out of the water all the time.

"It's all air around here," said Hob.

"Got to keep in training," said the spider.

"But why aren't you in a pond?" asked Hob. "There's a good big one behind the house."

"It's safer in here," said the spider. "The water there isn't quite right. I know there is something to eat in it, but it's much too large. I go down to the sink for water because I can only breathe air that has been wrapped up properly. It's much more ladylike and polite. Have you seen the people here? They breathe any air that's floating around. They don't wash it, they don't dry and polish it, they don't even keep a spare bubble or two. What if all the air dried up? What would they do then?"

"I came to borrow some silk," said Hob. "But I'd better look at the pond and find out what's wrong with it if that's where you are supposed to be."

"It's where I'd rather be," said the spider. "I've eaten everything else in the house. I suppose you haven't a tasty small fish on you? A small snack of some kind? To exchange for the silk."

But Hob had nothing like that with him. "Don't eat many of the children," he said. "I've counted them."

"Stay out of the pond," said the spider. "Believe me; I know." She went back behind the wardrobe.

When that was settled Hob had to find what work there was to do. That is his job.

"I must be getting lazy," he decided, after having

a good look around. "There's hardly anything to do. All the wrong things have left. I hope the house hasn't got a Hob already. That would be difficult because there's only me."

All he could find was a SlyMe, hiding in the drainpipe under the kitchen sink.

"Now then," said Hob, talking down the plug hole. "Can I help you on your way, SlyYou?"

"Please," said the SlyMe, "I'd like to go, really I would, because there isn't enough space here. But I daren't go out of the drain. Do you know where I would end up?"

"I can guess, SlyYou," said Hob. "In the pond."

"There's something in there," said SlyMe.

"People say it's treasure," said Hob.

"Treasure?" said SlyMe. "No, the very opposite. You wouldn't send a SlyMe down there, would you?"

"This does want thinking about," said Hob. "Stay where you are for now. But in the end I have my duty to do. Just don't make anyone ill."

SlyMe gurgled in his pipe. Hob went to sit by the fire and smoke his.

He looked around for an unnoticeable cupboard to sleep in, but they were all used up. There was not even a forgotten shelf. At last he climbed into the loft, under the roof, and found an empty place where jackdaws had dug into the thatch and left a good cutch that no one had dusted for a hundred years. Or a thousand, he thought. And there he curled up and went to sleep as day began.

Chapter Six

THE NEXT NIGHT Hob found a raisin cake in a blue bowl waiting for him in the fender. "They do understand," he said. "I wonder if they've had a Hob before. Something left for me in a blue bowl is exactly right."

He ate the raisin cake. He smoked his pipe. The clock went tick, the fire went out. That was all as it should be.

"Good raisin cake," said Hob. "As it should be."

"But," said Hob. "I really want something else. I long for something else."

That was not as it should be. Hob is glad of what he gets, thankful for what he is given. He thinks it is plenty. He does not like to be teased and have unkind tricks played on him, but if he gets what he likes he is happy.

So it is not his way to long for more when he has had good raisin cake.

"I want something else," he said. "I don't want to but I do. What am I going to do about it?"

He was nearest to the kitchen sink. He got up on the draining board and looked down the drain for SlyMe, and called to him. "SlyYou," he called.

"Yes," said SlyMe.

"I'm unhappy," said Hob. "I'm unhappy because

I am ungrateful and haven't been given the right thing, and that isn't like me at all."

"I'm unhappy, too," said SlyMe. "Hiding in this pipe all the time. I'd rather be crawling around the house making things yucky so people find it and call my name. 'Look how slimy,' they shout. I love that. But I daren't come out into the house, and I daren't be washed down the drain out of it."

Hob told SlyMe how he would like the thing he longed for. "Poached, maybe," he said. "On toast."

"Sorry," said SlyMe. "I can't talk about things like that. Please don't mention it again."

"But I haven't said what it is," said Hob.

"Don't," said SlyMe. "Go away and think about other food. We get hiccups with those things."

Hob climbed upstairs, still longing. He found the spider behind the wardrobe, blowing silvery bubbles.

"Blow your own," she said, taking a sniff from one of hers. "I can't spare any. What do you want?"

"Something fried," said Hob. "Or boiled, with bread and butter. Or just raw, on the shell. Hob likes an . . ."

The spider was so shocked she dropped all her bubbles of air and they broke on the floor.

"See what you made me do," she said. "Now there's air everywhere and I shan't be able to breathe, you silly Hob."

"But I haven't said anything," said Hob. "What's wrong with talking about . . ."

But the spider would not let him finish. "Stop it at once," she said. "Don't mention those things. You really are the most tiresome person, coming in here and spilling all my air so thoughtlessly. And you are about to say quite the wrong thing for this house." She stretched out a leg with a claw full of sticky spiderweb and stuck Hob's lips together.

"In this house," she went on, "we do not mention certain things, we don't eat them, we don't lay them, we don't cook them, we don't hatch them, and we don't bring them here. Understand?"

"But why?" asked Hob.

"You're going red in the face, Hob," said the spider. "I expect it's lack of air. We don't mention those things because."

"Because of what?" Hob tried to ask.

"You're going black in the face," said the spider. "I said, 'because,' and that's enough reason. But mostly because of the hiccups."

She went back to filling bubbles with air and packing them safely in her web.

"You don't suppose I would live here if there was somewhere better to go, do you?" she said, between breaths from her best bubbles.

"I have to live here," said Hob. "Until they send me away. I just long for a special treat."

"I'd send you away now," said the spider. "You're trouble, you are, Hob."

Hob went away. "If I can't eat them," he said to himself, "or speak about them," he muttered, "or even think about them," he thought, "well, it's very strange. It's something I shall look into. But surely someday . . ."

When he looked into the cupboards in the kitchen

there were plates and mugs and dishes and saucers and jugs and basins and jars and vases.

"Not a single eggcup," he said, without thinking.

At the moment he said the word "egg," the floor jumped under him, dust fell from the ceiling, SlyMe gurgled in his pipe, the spider dropped heavy air on the floor again, the children woke up screaming, Sally fell out of bed, the clock struck one and a half, Pyke fell off her perch, the door flew open, and George came running downstairs. Out he went and in he came.

"Oh, dear," he was saying. "Whose fault is it?"

"That was a hiccup," said Hob to himself. "This isn't how I behave at all. That was a mistake."

"Who said it?" said George. "Who did?"

"We were asleep," said the children.

"I said it," said Hob. "I was told not to, but I did. Sorry." No one heard him.

"It's careless dreaming," said George. "We can't manage all our dreams, but we must try hard."

"Hard," said Hob, quietly. "That's a good way. Hard-boiled would be perfect. Cold, with salt."

"I thought there must be a ship, at first," said George. "That the river had come back, working again. The water of the pond shook and splashed, and it never does that, so I had to watch."

"I wish we could live somewhere else," said Sally.

Hob thought that was a good idea. Somewhere with an ordinary house full of Damplings, Chair Ache, Unhappy Landings, and LampShade, where the lamps give off dark, not bright.

"I could get my teeth into a good dose of putting things right," he said to himself. "But here there is nothing. The house thinks it is perfect. There are no interesting bits left, except SlyMe and the spider. All the rest have gone, not even DoorMice squeaking when the door opens."

He knew that was unnatural. "That isn't how things are," he said. "But there, I am always longing for things I can't have, like a few little problems. They are my work. If there aren't any, no wonder my mind thinks of a better tea. So I'd better watch what I do. It would be very bad if I got HobSick, or HobNailed."

Now that everybody had got up, Sally woke the fire for a cup of tea and some raisin cake.

Hob climbed into the fender. They remembered him. They handed down cake and tea.

"The fire smells different," said George.

"That is Hob's pipe," said the children.

"No nonsense," said George.

"The peddler brought him in," said Michael.

"We asked him into the house," said Katie.

"There was nothing useful in the bundle," said George. "It was a joke of the peddler's. I expect it was funny, but I don't know why."

"But I am here," said Hob.

"We can't see him anymore," said the girl. "But it was a good joke while it lasted."

For a little while Hob was sad about not being there, until he remembered that he was.

"Time to go to bed again," said George. "Farming

is early daytime and late nighttime."

They went back to bed. Hob stayed in the fender and wondered why he was here. Being anywhere is not an accident. Something means it to happen. Something that hadn't yet happened itself had brought Hob here.

"I don't know what," he told the fire. "There isn't anything to look after."

SlyMe heard him. He called out in his gurgle voice, his climbing-up-a-pipe voice. "Hob," he said, "there is plenty for you to do. If you get rid of me you won't kill me, but if the thing outside catches me, then it will. It has got rid of everything else, so you will have to get rid of it."

"Yes," said Hob. "That is the problem. It is a big problem, and Hob only deals with little ones."

"It is not a big problem," said the spider, coming all the way down the stairs. "Give me some air. Thanks, that's better. No, it is not a little problem, nor a big problem, but a huge problem. And I think you came here to solve it."

"How big?" asked Hob.

"As big as – what do you think, SlyMe?" asked the spider. "How big is it?"

"As big as the sea," said SlyMe. "They say that won't fit in a bucket."

"That," said the spider, "depends on the size of the bucket. Can you get a big one, Hob?"

"I'll look around," said Hob. "If that's my work."

He sat beside the fire's last star, and when it had closed its eye he went to his own bed to close his.

Chapter Seven

HOB WOKE UP LATE in the evening. George and Sally were having a last cup of tea before going to bed. Hob crept into the fender and had a cup with them.

Hob had his tea and ate his bread. He sat on by the fire, smoking a thoughtful pipe.

"There's nothing I can do in the house," he said.

"Are you tick-tock-talking to me?" the clock seemed to say.

"No," said Hob. "Though it's about time."

"Are you going out?" said the fire. "I am."

"Yes," said Hob. "Those children are not asleep. They are thinking and listening, not dreaming properly, and I wonder why they are looking out the window. I shall go out and see what they are looking at and listening to."

Hob walked through the garden. He wondered what was wrong with it, because there was something unusual. Hob thought it was too quiet, like the house. But far away there was a sound that he did not know, that he had never heard before.

"No caterpillars," he said. "No one is eating anything. No holes in the leaves, no earwigs in the

roses. Perhaps that is why there are no birds here."
He was wrong about that, but there was no one to
tell him until after the last thing happened.

"Only that magpie," said Hob.

Hob looked at the water in the pond, very flat and
still. Nothing floated in it. It was quiet.

"The stars are reflected better than real," Hob said
to himself. "But I don't know which star is which."
He went to see what else was happening.

George was walking about on the edge of the pond
farthest from the house, watching gently.

"There was a river here once," he said. "It went past
quick and busy, with things floating in it, branches and
weeds and grass, swimming to the sea."

"A dark night," said Hob. "A sky full of clouds."

George heard him. "No moon or stars," he said.
"I can hear something," he said. "Something from
long ago."

"Something is not right," said Hob. "But George
knows best, so I will say nothing."

Hob was trying to explain to himself why there
were no stars in the sky, though he could see their
reflections in the pond. "I don't suppose it is my
business," he said. "That's what it'll be – not my
business. A Hob's life is a hard one, full of puzzles
and things he can't understand."

A door banged at the house. Children called.
Michael and Katie came running through the dark
in their nightgowns.

"We heard it coming," said Michael. "Wait for us.

We are going with you."

"Don't leave without us," said Katie.

"We are not going anywhere," said George. "But I have heard it, too."

At that moment, even though the children were chattering and jumping about, Hob heard it quite clearly, too, and saw it coming along.

"A ship," he said. "It is a ship, coming down the river that is not there, coming from long ago, floating in the air, but thinking it is in the water, and getting wet from it."

"Ship ahoy," said George. He waved his lantern. "At last, a ship."

"Time has slipped a bit," said Hob. "It's meant to. Backward, forward, sideways. It goes around and around the clock face, so it is going around and around here. I expect I have been sleeping backward again."

The ship was floating through the fields. Men were sailing and steering it. There was a lantern high on its mast. On its deck men were singing songs of the sea to the tune of a fiddle.

"Ship ahoy," called George.

"Ship ahoy," called Michael.

"Stop and we shall come with you," Katie shrieked. Hob looked and listened.

"Ahoy there," someone called from the ship. "We are lost because the stars we steer by are all wrong. Can we sail through to the sea?"

"There is no sea here," George called back. "The sea has gone. There is a pond, but no sea."

"The sea was there before," said the sailor.

"It is always somewhere," said George. "Here it is all land now."

"They obviously don't know about the sea," said Hob to himself. "It creeps up behind you suddenly and gets you wet. And there are big things swimming in it."

The ship came very close. It was longer than a house. Hob did not know how the water stayed out. But he remembered that some things will float in the kitchen sink, like the empty shells of . . . and he nearly said the word out loud. It was just ready to be said. It was in his mouth, ready to come out. He nearly hatched it on his tongue.

At that moment the water in the pond stopped being calm. It rippled and bubbled, and the ground quivered under his feet. The pond seemed to be about to behave like the sea, about to creep up behind Hob and get him wet.

"Snails," said Hob. "I was going to say snails."

The water stopped rippling. The ground growled and kept still. Hob forgot about eggs.

"We're sailing on by," said the sailor on the ship. "We can't tie up here in any case. The riverbank is too shaky."

"It is quite safe," called Michael. "Wait, wait."

"We have to go with you," Katie shouted. "Let us into your ship."

"Oh, wait," thought Hob. "Wherever you are going I want to follow, to all the new places." He had seen work going past, lovely work that he longed to do. He had seen a home he would very much like, but it had floated by. He had seen a ship with a thousand things ready to be put right, and with dozens of cutches to choose from. But all the thousand things had sailed by.

The ship floated over the pond without touching it, crossed the road, swung through the trees, sailing the air to the sea. On board the crew went on with their songs, and the fiddle gave the tune.

"I'm going in to bed," said George. "Good night, whoever you are, and prosperous voyage."

The ship had not been quite real. There was no river; there had been no ship.

But it had been real enough for Michael to wipe his nose on his sleeve, and for Katie to cling to her father and cry nearly enough saltwater for any ship.

"I'm not sure about the singing, perhaps," thought Hob. "But I should be busy from night to morn putting things right, pulling out wormholes, plumping up the ropes so they are comfy to sit on, ironing the sails so the wind doesn't get into them, making holes in the bottom of the ship to let the water out when it comes in over the top. I would make a good sailor. A cabin Hob."

No one had invited him aboard. He had to stay where he was, on land, with the sea nowhere near.

Morning was coming. "Well," said Hob to himself, "I've been here all night and it's time to go to bed. The children should have been in long ago."

George was taking them home, telling them that it had been a dream from the past, when the pond had been a deep part of the river and the sea had washed the front doorstep with salt.

Hob followed them and went up to the loft. It was bedtime for him. Before that there was one task left. One sad star was tucked in beside Sootkin in the chimney. Hob took her outside, lifted her up in her shawl of night, and sent her up into the sky.

She flew up, and up, the only light there was, and went behind a cloud.

$$\downarrow$$

—————— *Chapter Eight* ——————

Next morning Hob was going to bed when the children were being woken up. They said it was too early.

"You've had a good night's sleep," said Sally. "If you don't get up now you will never be ready."

Hob did not know what they would not be ready for. "They don't want to be ready for it, I can tell," he said. "But it's my job to go to sleep now, so Good Morning, house, everyone in it. And the pond."

So he went to sleep. He slept until the end of the daylight, and then he got up.

"I'm getting used to the house," he said. "That's what. And it's such a quiet house. I wonder where the children were all day. They generally wake me up at least once, clattering about, pulling each other's hair, or falling downstairs."

Hob went for his breakfast. The rest of the family thought it was tea beside the fire.

There was a cup of tea ready for Hob.

"I don't know why you put a saucer down in the fender," said George. "We haven't got a cat."

"We've got a Hob," said Sally. "Remember."

"Nonsense," said George. "And I do believe there's

a cup in that saucer."

"Of course, George," said Sally.

Hob picked up the cup and sipped his tea. Katie handed him a piece of toast with sardines and cucumber on it. Hob took it, politely.

He smelled the bread, the butter, the pepper, the sardines, the cucumber. But Katie smelled different. Michael smelled different.

"Not clean, or dirty," said Hob to himself. "But Katie smells of ink, and Michael smells of chalk. What funny stuff to play with."

Sally was asking them what sort of day they had had, and what they had learned.

Michael and Katie said it had been an awful day and they hadn't learned anything.

"I learned something every day when I was at school," said George. "Have you done seven times seven yet?"

"No," said Michael. "That's in the top class."

"I haven't even done seven," said Katie. "I'm too young. They've got it locked up in a cupboard."

"Best place for it," said Hob. "Big ugly number like that."

"We were tired all day," said Michael.

"From being awake all night," said Katie.

"Now, don't be silly," said their mother. "You were tucked up in bed. I saw you."

"They weren't," said Hob to himself. "They were out watching a ship come sailing by."

"We wanted the ship to anchor in the pond,"

said Michael.

"And take us on an adventure," said Katie.

"Or give us treasure," said Michael.

"Oh, dear," said Sally. She felt their foreheads. "You're hot," she said. "I think you have a fever coming on, and you are talking wildly."

"But you told us about the ships bringing elephants and boxes of gold," said Michael. "The ship was full of them."

"That was a hundred years ago," said Sally.

"A thousand," said George.

"It was last night," said Michael.

"It was, it was," said Hob. No one heard him, but he got a second cup of tea.

The children went to bed early that night, when the smell of school ink and the dust of chalk had been washed off them.

"Well, that's all over and done with," said Hob. "They'll be playing all day long tomorrow and I'll be the one who doesn't get much sleep."

He was surprised to find that the children went to school every day. "Learning dangerous stuff like seven," Hob told the magpie, when he was going to his cutch and she was waking for the day.

"The right number for a family," said Pyke. "Some to fall out of the nest and some to stay in."

Later that day there was a worse noise than children. The magpie had come into the house and Sally was chasing it out with a broom. But Pyke knew what she wanted.

"Stop it, ow," she was calling, while Sally waved the broom.

"Go out, you horrible bird," Sally was shouting.

"No," said Pyke. "I must wake Hob."

"And stop squawking," said Sally. "I can't understand a word you're saying."

The magpie flew around the ceiling. She flew up the stairs. She came up the loft ladder. Sally did not follow her.

"Find your own way out," Sally called. "And stay out."

Hob sat up. "What do you want?" he asked.

"Get to work, Hob," said Pyke. "If you didn't sleep all day you'd know what was happening."

"I don't," said Hob. "I do night, not day."

"Those chatterbox children," said Pyke. "They have nothing better to do at school but gossip to their friends, and the friends talk to everybody, and soon the news is all over the place."

"That's how it spreads," said Hob. "If everyone told the truth the news would be better, but not so exciting. But they haven't any to tell. They just come home smelling of ink and strange numbers."

"They talked about the ship," said Pyke. "They talked about treasure."

"Oh," said Hob. "But why are you waking me to tell me that? It has nothing to do with me. I have no use for treasure. I don't go to shops to buy things, so I don't need it. Money is only buttons, and I have no buttonholes."

"You are very stupid, Hob," said Pyke. "You are here to help George look after the pond. There are men coming to take treasure out of the pond."

"They can have it," said Hob. "All they have to leave behind is the water. Then they have the treasure, which is what they want, and we have the pond to go on looking after. What's the problem?"

Pyke was angrily pulling pieces of thatch out of the roof and absentmindedly building a nest on a beam. She was too cross to speak.

"So I'll go back to sleep," said Hob.

"If you don't come out with me and do something about it," she said, with her beak full of nest, "then I'll come and live in here next to you and when you snore I'll nip your nose."

"Good snore is a sign of good sleeping," said Hob.

"You're awake now," said Pyke. "Come out to the pond at once."

Hob got up. He climbed downstairs. He got out of the door safely, but Pyke was chased around the kitchen twice.

"Nasty thieving bird," Sally called after her. The magpie had taken a jam tart, fresh from the oven, so hot she burned her tongue.

By the pond were three men and the two very big farmhorses Mammoth and Mastodon. There was a net and a heavy piece of iron. The men intended to drag the net across the pond and pull treasure up from the bottom.

"Stop them," said Pyke.

"Yes," said Hob. He thought he could do it. "I know horse language, and they'll understand."

He hurried around to the horses. They stood patiently, nodding to one another, happy to stand still, thinking about grass and oats and being combed and brushed and groomed, and how they had been three times Best in Show. Horses are proud.

Hob climbed a rope and walked across the back of Mastodon. His back wrinkled when he felt Hob.

"Something tickling my back, Mammoth," he said.

"Imagination," said Mammoth. "Can't see it."

Mastodon whisked his tail up over his back, and Hob was knocked to the ground.

"That's better," said Mastodon.

"But listen," Hob shouted, down between their hairy ankles.

Mammoth shuffled his feet. "Don't want to tread on it," he said. "Something talking."

"Best stamp on it," said Mastodon. "There are tricky things near water."

Hob stood in front of them both, where he would not be tread upon. "Please listen," he shouted.

Both big heads bent to look at him.

"Nothing there," said Mammoth, "but it talks."

"What do you want, gossip?" said Mastodon.

"It'll be one of those will-o'-the-wisp things," said Mammoth. "I ate one once. It gave me hiccups."

"Please listen," said Hob. "This is important."

"We aren't doing anything," said Mastodon. "So say what you want."

"Tell them," said Pyke. But that was all she had time to say. The men had fixed the net, and they were ready to drag it through the pond.

"Hy-yup," one of them called. "Walk forward, Mammoth, Mastodon."

"Sorry," said Mammoth. "Lovely talk, but we have to work. Visit us again when we aren't busy."

Both horses pulled with their shoulders, and the net began to go into the pond.

"What will happen to us now?" shrieked Pyke. "It is the end of the world."

Chapter Nine

THE ROPES WERE TIGHTENING. "How-how," called one of the men. They talked about great treasure to each other. They had heard many a time, they said, that it was hidden in this pond and must be valuable.

They were not thinking of the end of the world.

Hob was thinking of the end of the world. "It'll be very interesting," he said. "But where shall I go then? And would I understand it? I don't understand the beginning of it."

"Hob, say something," called Pyke.

"Stop," said Hob to the horses. But Mammoth and Mastodon were taking a step forward, one hoof at a time, and pulling hard with three others at the same time. Their shoulders were heavy with work.

"Say the word," said Pyke.

"I've forgotten about horses," said Hob. "I don't know the word. I could stop a mouse, if we had one. All you have to do is say . . ."

Pyke was stamping about in the grass, tearing it up with her beak, angry at not being able to do anything useful, furious because Hob did not help. "Say that other word."

"Which word?" said Hob. "I know several words, and I think I could say them all anywhere. What's your problem, and what word is it?"

"Oh," said Pyke. "It was on the tip of my beak. It's one of those things in a shell."

"Oh, a nut," said Hob. "A walnut or a hazelnut?"

"Neither," said Pyke, crossly. "It's another thing in a shell, quite different."

"I remember," said Hob. "A snail, of course."

"No," said Pyke, leaping up and down and flapping her wings. "You should be able to remember a simple word, Hob."

Mammoth and Mastodon took another step each. The net began to touch the water at the other side of the pond. The men shouted encouragement.

"Tell me which one," said Hob. "If it's so easy."

"A shell all around it," said Pyke. "The shell wraps it up so you can carry it about."

"Of course," said Hob. "You mean oysters."

Pyke was too angry to speak now. She fluttered about on the grass among the horses' legs.

"You'll get trampled," said Mastodon.

"It won't be our fault," said Mammoth. "We're just obeying orders."

"People lay them in nests," said Pyke.

"They don't," said Hob. "Birds do. You are thinking of things I don't know about. I must stop playing games and do something about these horses."

"Please," said Pyke.

Hob knew then what word he ought not to say.

It was the word no one was to say around here, around the house, around the pond. He knew it so well that it wasn't there for him to say, specially if he thought about it. Hob is careful about these things.

"Hob is careful about these things," said Hob.

"What do birds lay?" shouted Pyke. "Will you please say the word?"

"Hi, hi," shouted one of the men. "Pull, pull."

"Mammoth, Mammoth," shouted another.

"Mastodon, Mastodon," shouted the third.

The net was going under the black water. The water was thinking about that, heaping itself up into a little wave, shivering all over, wrinkling, looking more than moody, looking offended.

"Something dreadful will happen," said Pyke.

"The end of the world," said Hob. "There'll be a lot of tidying up to do, and that's Hob's work."

"The word," said Pyke.

"All right," said Hob. "One of them, or a lot?"

"A lot," said Pyke. "Some are sure to fall out of the nest, but some will stay in."

"Seven eggs," said Hob. "Eggs, eggs, eggs."

When he said the word before there had been noises and shaking of the ground, hiccup in fact.

Now there were noises and shaking of the ground. Hiccup again, or just feeling slightly too full?

The horses were pulling hard when a spout of water lifted the net into the air. It whirled about and fell down again. Water splashed heavily back into water. The net dropped on the three men and tangled them up. Darkness leaped out of the pond.

Mammoth and Mastodon went on pulling. Ropes to the net were still hitched to them. No one told them to stop when the ground shook under them.

"Getting the work done," said Mammoth.

"Really plowing now," said Mastodon.

"Tough field, boyo," said Mammoth.

"Getting there," said Mastodon.

They pulled the men through the pond. They pulled them beyond it. No one told them to stop.

"A long field," Hob heard Mammoth say as they went out of sight.

"There's our stable," said Mastodon.

"Must be going home," said Mammoth.

Hob thought he was alone. The ground had been shaken so hard that grass was upside down. Trees slept with their heads on a pillow of hedge.

Near the house the children had been climbing a stile, and it had jumped under them like a horse. They did not want it to stop.

The shaking and the noise were over. The pond settled down again and was almost still. At the edge of it something struggled in a muddy place.

Hob went to pick it up. "Fishy things drown in the air." He was being kind. "I'll throw you into the middle." The thing nipped him sharply.

"Leave me alone," it said. "See what you did, saying that word."

It was Pyke, wet and dirty, cross because Hob wanted to throw her into the pond, but pleased that he had said the right word at last.

"It drove the men away," she said.

"It's only a pond," said Hob.

"It's a pond on top," said Pyke. "It's what's in there that matters. Didn't the peddler tell you?"

"No one told me," said Hob. "What am I looking after?"

"It's like this," said Pyke. "Long ago . . . but now the children are coming and they're sure to chase me, so I'll have to tell you another time."

She flew away lopsided, half her feathers full of water and half full of mud.

"She is horrible," said Hob. "But she is brave, too. I wish I knew what I am meant to do, and why the pond has to be watched, and how to watch it, and what it is like underneath."

That was wrong, he thought. "Hob should know what he is doing," he said. "Hob is not children."

The children ran from the house. Sally sent them out because the house had filled with dust when the ground shook, and she was having to sweep and tidy.

"Housekeeping goes on all the time," the magpie said to her from the window. Sally threw a brush at her, thinking it was all probably her fault.

"I wish it was," said the magpie, flying off and telling Hob. "It would serve her right."

George came to the pond after the children. The children ran around it, and George watched.

"Don't touch," he said. "I thought we weren't going to have these troubles with a Hob to help us.

I hope he isn't causing them."

"Oh, he is," said Pyke. But George did not know her language.

The sky became patchy with night, and one star appeared in a bit of day that was still there.

"It's the teapot star," said Hob. "When it comes out so does the teapot. It's time to go in."

"I didn't finish telling you about the pond," said Pyke.

"It'll do tomorrow," said Hob. "I want my cup of tea and a little nod by the fire indoors. I'm an indoor person, and Hob will never understand ponds. They don't teach them at school, and I didn't go to school anyway, so how can I know about them?"

By the fire indoors Sally was saying, "But that is where the trouble is. I blame that magpie. It came into the house and then went to the pond and there was that earthquake. The bird was looking in at the window again until I chased it off. Get the peddler to take it away."

"But she's Hob's friend," said Katie.

"She talks to him," said Michael.

"My friend?" thought Hob. "No, not at all."

His cup of tea, which he had been enjoying until that moment, tipped itself over in its saucer and flooded the fender.

"Oh, dear," said Sally. "The teapot's dribbling again."

But Katie said, "Perhaps we said the wrong thing."

And Michael said, "Maybe the magpie is not Hob's friend. We are sorry, Hob."

A buttered biscuit came down to Hob's hand. The teapot dribbled more tea into his cup.

"Just a little sleep," said Hob. "Then off to work for the night."

Chapter Ten

THERE WAS NOT MUCH WORK to do that night. This was a house that all the slightly wrong things had left, and there was not much to do. "It's not healthy to have nothing wrong with you," Hob said. "That's as plain as an invisible nose on an invisible face."

Only SlyMe sat in the sink drain. Only the Giant Water Spider lived quietly under the wardrobe, wrapping her bubbles of air in case of a shortage.

"It's the pond," Hob told himself. "I'm not a pond person. They have fins and tails like fish."

He went to bed when Sally and the children got up. He did not sleep at all well. Michael and Katie were at school, so they were not keeping him awake.

Hob should have been asleep, not thinking about the children, wondering why they liked coming home with ink on their fingers and chalk in their hair and smelling of both.

Sally was baking and making and dusting and polishing.

"Tonight there will be something good to eat," thought Hob. "But I should not be lying here in my cutch thinking about that either."

Outside George was gardening. His spade was gently turning the earth over. He was sprinkling water on the flowers and herbs. He was singing gently to himself.

"That did not wake me," thought Hob.

Pyke was on the roof. She laughed to herself a bit. Probably something unkind had happened to another bird and she thought it was funny. Then she tried to laugh again, but nothing funny was happening.

"She is trying to cheer herself up in her cruel way," thought Hob. "That is not what woke me up. That is not keeping me awake."

He turned over in his cutch, where he should have been comfortable in the thatch. Pyke was outside the roof, talking to herself.

"She is not happy," said Hob. "I am not happy. I will get up and look around. Sally and George are happy. The children are playing at ink. But there is something not quite right."

He got out of the cutch and went downstairs. Sally was rolling pastry. George came in.

"It is beginning to rain," he said. "The wind is getting up."

"The kitchen fire is not burning its best," said Sally. "The wind got up on the wrong side of the bed."

"We are going to have bad weather," said George. The fire was sulking.

"Wake up," said Hob. "I am awake."

"Don't feel well," said the fire. "I am crying."

The tear it had felt was only a drop of rain down the chimney, making a black kiss on the red heat.

"It's getting dark," said Sally.

"Rain will do the garden good," said George.

Hob went out to see what was going on. Worms were leaving home, writhing and writing wriggly messages as they went. Hob could not read those messages.

"It must be the pond," he said. "That's what it says, in big letters."

The pond was not doing anything that Hob could see. It was dark there, and the water lay quiet and flat, even where drops of rain splashed in.

"There you are," said Pyke. She was sitting under a tree. "I suppose this is all your fault, Hob. Why are you dreaming this bad dream? Why can't you leave me out of it? I am a pensioner, and you ought not to dream me."

Pyke herself did not dream. She thought people had dreams on purpose to put other people in them and make them unhappy.

Hob sat down in the rain to think about things. He tried to light his pipe because that would help him. But first the wind and then the rain put that out. He only got one puff of smoke, and that fell at his feet and hid under a leaf.

Hob does not mind rain. It goes straight through him if he wants it to. He says to himself that he is not really there, so of course he can't get wet. Only his pipe won't burn.

"I'd better get into shelter," he said to Pyke. "My pipe is a thinking pipe."

"Go up on the roof first," said Pyke. "Look at the sea."

Hob told Pyke he thought the sea was a whole day's journey away by donkey-cart.

"It is a very slow donkey," said Pyke. "Now go up and look."

Hob climbed the house wall, up on the prickly branches of a rose bush. He climbed onto the thatch. He did not like being up so high, and thatch is not meant for walking on. It is smooth and steep, and he slipped and slithered.

Pyke pulled him by one ear.

They climbed to the chimney. Hob held onto it and looked down it. There was Sootkin, clinging to the sides. The smoke was not coming out. It sat inside, saying it was afraid.

"There is nothing to be afraid of," said Hob.

He stood up beside the chimney and looked around about. He had to hold on so that the wind did not tear him away. He could be afraid of falling off.

Down below there was the garden. There was George's wheelbarrow, turned up against the wall. There was the garden gate, rattling on its latch. At the bottom of the garden was the pond. There was a great deal of darkness there, as if the night had stayed beyond its time.

Hob looked another way. There were farm buildings and fields, and trees, and beyond them another house with a bell.

"That's the school," said Pyke. "With the bell. Look

the other way."

"Fields," said Hob. "I'm not a field person. Field persons live in gateways and furrows and ditches. I am an indoor house person, not a creeper-crawler."

"Look," said Pyke. "Shall I get George's glasses? I am good at picking and stealing."

Hob looked without glasses. He had thought that the fields went on a long way and out of sight. He stared, and saw the sea beyond, a few fields away.

"I thought it was trees dancing," he said.

"No," said Pyke. "It is waves eating the land. The sea is coming through the fields. It is washing them away."

"Sally said it once came as far as the house," said Hob. "Is it coming again? And does it matter? Won't the house still be here? Houses are safe."

"Look again," said Pyke. "What else can you see? Do you still think the house will be here?"

Hob looked again. He saw waves jumping on the edge of the land. He saw them leaping into the air, higher than any house, and heard them crashing down.

"That kept me awake," he said. "Not enough to hear inside, but enough to stop me from sleeping."

Over the sea there were black clouds. Under them there was lightning, hopping from sky to sea, flashing from cloud to cloud. Hob heard it sizzling like a sausage in a frying pan, the bright sparks like the fat that leaps out and burns in the fire.

"The sea is on fire," he said. "Wet and burning."

"Is there anything else?" asked Pyke.

Hob looked beyond the waves, beyond the

lightning. Something large swam across the sea, lifting its head, opening its mouth, waving its fins.

"Might be teeth," said Hob. "On a sea animal. I never have to think of sea animals. It has come up to look at the storm."

"All the same," said Pyke, "I am going to hide in a safe place."

"It will not hurt me," said Hob. "But I will come down at once." He looked down the chimney. Sally was saying there would be nothing to eat with the fire like this. The smoke was still cowering in the flue, too frightened to come out.

"Well," thought Hob, "something to do at last." He put his hand in, took hold of the smoke by its collar, dragged it out and sent it off into the wind. Once it had started it could not stop, and away it romped. Down below the fire woke up and felt cheerful. Sally said, "About time, too."

A huge puff of wind knocked Hob from the ridge of the roof. He slid down the thatch. Pyke was beside him, knocked down, too.

Overhead there was a snap of lightning. Pyke straightened her feathers when the lightning had fluffed them all up. The hair on Hob's back went prickle-twitch-prickle, ticklish for him. He laughed. Nobody tickles Hob, but he likes it.

"Don't laugh," said Pyke.

"The lightning told a sparky joke," said Hob. "Now the sky will laugh."

The sky did laugh. The thunder rumbled right

around the land. There was another sparky joke, and more guffawing, all over the sky.

Hob hurried down the rose bush and scampered across the grass to the tipped-up wheelbarrow. He sat underneath that. He lit his pipe. He thought about things. He listened to the concert of thunder. He went to sleep. Now he could hear noise he did not mind it.

Chapter Eleven

HOB HAD A DREAM, out in the rainy garden under the tipped-up wheelbarrow. He woke up very suddenly to see whether it was a true dream.

"It's because I am under something," he said.

He had dreamed dreadfully that he was in the huge mouth of an enormous creature, nipped among the teeth, ready to be swallowed.

"I have been in the mouth of a dog," he remembered. "It was wet, and that was all. I turned myself to a horrible taste and he let me go. This time I turned myself into waking up, and escaped."

He still had the dream in his head. He thought he would stay awake until it had left. Such a large mouth he had been in, so many teeth, and something roaring in the throat behind him, a tongue so long and wet and licking.

"I will think of other things," Hob thought. "It is still raining. I shall stay here and smoke my pipe."

The pipe was full of rain and would not burn. But Hob had a feeling of warm teapot in the house, and went to have a look. The teapot was by the fire. Hob sat beside it. He put his pipe to dry.

The children were home from school. Inky smell had been washed away by rain.

"It is the worst storm they have ever had," Michael said. "It is the highest tide, and the sea got into the fields."

"The cows had to swim to the shed," said Katie. "They were blowing bubbles."

Hob thought the cows would have been carrying air, like the Giant Water Spider.

"There will be a shipwreck," said Michael.

"I shall watch for sailors," said Katie. "They will need looking after."

How kind, thought Hob. He thought it again when a cup of tea and a slice of apple pie came down to him. Since his dream, he wondered what it was like for the pie to be in his mouth among his teeth, with his tongue all around it. The pie did not complain.

His dream went away. Probably the pie was having it. Hob lit his pipe.

"Chimney still smoking," said George, rattling the fire up with the poker through the bars.

"Let it have its fun," said Sally.

"It's Hob," said Katie.

Hob went to sleep, comfortable by the fire.

He woke up when everything was quiet. The wind and storm had gone away.

"I will go around the house," said Hob, "and see that everything is all right."

SlyMe was asleep. Hob heard his gurgling snore. He sounded healthy, and bigger than he had been.

He had lots of rich washing-up water on baking days.

The Giant Water Spider was interested to hear about cows blowing bubbles. "I hope there's still enough air to go around," she said. "Share and share alike."

Hob went into the loft. The thatch was heavy with rain. The house had a slight headache from it.

Windows downstairs had been dazzled by lightning. They did not have headache, but WindowPain.

Hob blinked their curtains across, to close them all.

Upstairs the children dreamed about the sea and the beach.

Outside Hob heard singing from across the fields, dancing and a violin. He heard the sounds skipping in the children's dreams.

"I hope they do not wake up frightened," he thought. "But who is in the fields?"

The children dreamed that singing was on the beach, that dancing was on the rocks, that the violin was calling to them.

"You are singing me awake, Michael," said Katie.

The song was a song of the sea, "Hey Ho, Blow the Man Down," or "Across the Roaring Forties." Children enjoy songs from far away.

They wanted to hear the songs from up close. They got up out of their beds and crept downstairs, out of the door and into the fields along a path.

Hob could not catch them up. They ran through field after field, right to the edge of the sea.

There, stranded in a high and salty hedge, was a wrecked ship, standing in the moonlight, with her sails

torn, the anchor dangling, the lantern crooked.
The sailors were singing but not dancing. They
were singing to help them mend the ship.

They were patching sails and tying ropes,
scrubbing decks and brightening brass, drying
the cargo and lifting the hatches.

The captain was sighting the moon with his
instruments to find out where they were. The doctor
was tending a cabin boy with a bruised head. The
carpenter was down in the hedge looking for holes.

"We have come to help," said the children.

"You shall sail with us," the captain said. "Learn
our songs and all the knots a sailor has to know."

"I shall have to stop that," Hob thought. "Those
children belong at home, and at school." But he had
other things to do for now. The easy things that
people knew about he left to them. Things they
could not see he had to deal with.

"I don't think I would ever get time to sleep on
a ship," he said to himself. "There are a thousand
things that I understand how to put right. There are a
thousand things I do not understand, and they ought
to be put right, too. For a start, it would be better if the
ship was the other way up, then the rain would not get
in. I think they have built the roof underneath. And it
would be better to have the sails underwater, so the
ship could be pushed along by gentle sea currents.
I would cure the sea of Rough. The sails could catch
fish for supper as well."

But he could not interfere. There might be a good

reason for having the ship that way up. "It could be easier when they land in a hedge," he thought. "If they meant to land in the hedge."

"Shipwrecked, Miss," a sailor was telling Katie.

"Seeking the current and the tide, and the old river-mouth." said the captain. "And the stars all wrong."

"Between the shore and the thing in the sea," said the cook. "There it was, as big as an island."

"And its mouth open," said the captain.

"Counting its teeth, I was," said the cook.

Katie and Michael shivered when they were told these things. "Is it there now?" they asked.

"Swam away," said the captain. "Shouting loudly for its little one."

"Wanted its supper, I say," said the cook. "All those teeth. I know hungry when I see it."

The tide was rising up and the sea was in the hedge. It began to lift the ship.

"Yo heave ho," the sailors sang.

"All aboard," said the captain. "Are you coming?"

"Their mother will be shouting for her little ones," said Hob. He was busy routing out a Compass Beetle turning north to south in a naughty way.

"We have to go to school," said Katie. "It's not much fun and takes so long."

"But one day we'll come," said Michael.

The sea began to lift the ship. Michael helped his sister into the branches of a tree. The sailors pulled ropes and sang their chantey. The violin played faster, and the ship began to rock.

"What was the big thing in the sea?" called Michael.

"And how many teeth?" asked Katie. Hers were falling out and new ones growing.

"A mouthful," said the captain. "Here we go. Good-bye, and good-bye."

Hob jumped out at the last minute. He had not been invited to stay. He could not go.

"What was its name?" Michael was calling.

The ship lifted out of the hedge. The captain shouted back to Michael, but he did not hear.

"We shall never know," he said. The ship left the hedge, the field, the beach, and was at sea.

Hob had heard what the Captain shouted. He thought about it. "It's never going to matter to me," he said. "But it's not easy to forget."

Now he had to get the children home. Their dream had finished, and they wanted to be in bed. He led them through the dark. They sang little sailor songs as they walked.

Sally met them in the fields. She thought they should not have come out in the dark.

"You do not know what wild animals there are," she told them.

"There are no wild animals left," said Katie. "We were quite safe."

"And we were coming home," said Michael. "You did not need to worry."

"No need to worry," thought Hob, remembering what the captain had said, remembering his dream. "No wild animals? But what the sailors saw in the sea is what I saw, too. It was the Sea Serpent. And what is the Sea Serpent doing here?"

He did not know. But is there anything wilder?

Chapter Twelve

H OB WAS ALARMED AGAIN, later in the night.
The children were frightened, too. They
woke again, and Sally went to them, saying,
"Now this is too much. We have had enough
disturbance for one night."

Not cross, thought Hob, but not having any
nonsense. Just how I deal with little problems.

"If," he said, "this is a little problem."

The children had heard what Hob heard. They
did not know what was calling and howling away
across the fields, at the nearest sea to the house.

Hob knew what it must be. "The Sea Serpent,"
he told the Giant Water Spider.

She had heard it, too, and got ready all her bubbles
of air. "Something is about to change," she said. "Is it
going to be breakfast time?"

"Maybe," said Hob. "But what is for breakfast
and what is going to have it?"

After all, the Sea Serpent needs its food every day,
and breakfast is part of food. And very often in the
wild the last thing the food hears is the howling of
the thing that will eat it.

"But the noise," the children were saying.

"It is a cat," said Sally.

"It is a lion," said Michael.

"A tiger," said Katie.

"A sea lion," said George, coming to see whether to be cross with people at this time in the morning.

"Don't get its name right," said Hob. "That would really frighten you." But they did not hear him.

At the most dangerous moment they will, Hob thought. They will know the name, and what it is. But they will not know what to do. They will want me to tell them, but I do not know either.

Hob went looking for Pyke. She will know, he thought. She will have heard the noise.

Pyke was perched under the thatch at the end of the house. She had heard the noise. She opened one eye and looked at Hob. He was in the uncomfortable rose bush.

"Going on the roof?" she asked.

"You can hear what's going on," said Hob. "What are we doing about it?"

Pyke opened the other eye. "It's out at sea," she said. "Anyone can tell that. I'm not going to look. I'm not a seagull. I'm a retired magpie."

"I'll have to go down there again," said Hob. "Perhaps I ought to stay and look after the house."

Down by the sea something called. It was a noise like a hundred cows and a dozen lions.

"Go, I think," said Hob.

Inside the house Katie screamed.

"Stay, I think," said Hob.

"Don't go looking for trouble," said Pyke. "Or hang about waiting for it."

Hob held tighter onto a thorny twig. He thought the whole rose bush might be shaking in the ground. Pyke looked about her. She held on tightly to her perch.

At the shore something was hitting the land. The shaking came from that.

Pyke thought for a time. She walked up and down. She preened her feathers.

"No time for that," said Hob. "Sitting there trying to look nice."

"You don't know about birds," said Pyke. "That's what."

Hob knew about birds in houses. He thought they were not very sensible. But the magpie was different. She certainly had more brain. But why was a sensible bird smoothing her feathers and tidying herself when she ought to be thinking of helpful things to do?

"That's that," she said at last. "Now I'm ready."

She was smart and shining. Hob did not think that had anything to do with his problem. It didn't tell him what the problem was, and half of a problem is not knowing the other half. Or sometimes actually knowing it.

"I'll go indoors," he said. "Nothing useful is happening out here. I think you are vain."

"Please yourself," said Pyke. "But I can't fly long distances with important messages with my feathers rumpled. I would fall to the ground and be eaten by a fox. So would you."

"But we aren't going anywhere," said Hob. "I am going into the house, that is all. You are certainly not flying away with me."

"You stay here," said Pyke. "Hob can't leave until the house sends him away. But I am flying off to find the peddler. He will know what to do. Now do you understand?"

"Yes," said Hob. "You are a much wiser bird than most of the ones I have met."

"I am a lot older," said Pyke. "Stay here and keep things in order. The peddler will know what to do, and will come here as soon as possible."

She took a quick look at the sky to find the right guiding star. Then she took another look.

"This isn't any good," she said. "It's not cloudy tonight, so I can see the stars, and I ought to be able to steer by them. But they are all in the wrong place. I can't find my way to the peddler with them in that state."

Hob had been thinking that the peddler might not be a good idea. The peddler had been sly, and picked Hob up and sold him, so he couldn't be trusted. "But what can we do without him?" asked Hob.

"He knows what's what," said Pyke. "I think things are beginning to happen here."

"But if you can't find your way," said Hob, "how will he know there is a problem, and what it is?"

"I'm not proud," said Pyke. "If I can't find my way by the stars – and I don't know what's the matter with them; things were never like this when I was young – if the stars are broken, then I'll flutter like a sparrow, along the hedges and edges, by roadsides and ditches, until I find him."

She opened her wings and spread them wide.

"Mind the top of the cage," said Hob, because he was used to birds kept in the house.

"Nothing here I can't manage," said Pyke.

"The children are frightened," said Hob. "They have got NightScare and DayDread. They will not be happy whether it is light or dark."

"Go in and help them," said Pyke. "But I think your work is out here. I don't know what, but that's where the danger is."

Hob knew that was true, but since the danger was coming nearer, when it arrived would be his time to deal with it. "I'm a house person," he said. "I'll go in when you have gone."

"Wave me good-bye," said Pyke. "You might never see me again, and that would be sad." She smoothed a few last feathers, nodded at Hob, and flew into the air, up and out of sight.

"I'll go in," said Hob. "I didn't have time to wave and I can't see her in the dark."

But Pyke was down beside him at once. "It's happening," she said. "It's on the land. Go and look from the roof." Hob climbed the rose bush. He clambered onto the thatch. He crawled up it and came to the top. He stood by the chimney again.

Daylight was just beginning over the sea. A cold,

cold wind blew from there. A voice called out, not quite a word, but very likely a meaning.

"What does it say?" said Hob.

"It means," said Pyke, flying around his head, "it didn't say. It means that we shall have to give it back."

She flew away then. Hob saw her, black and white, against a dark sky. She flew over the garden and began to cross the pond.

"Give what back?" called Hob. "The sea? The land? The children?"

"None of those," called Pyke, from above the pond. "We must give back the . . ."

Hob did not hear what she said. While she was speaking the ground went bump and everything rattled. A spout of water from the pond fountained into the air, catching Pyke as she flew.

The water fell down again. There was no magpie.

There was only Hob on the roof, and in the house children crying under the bedclothes at the very foot of their beds.

Away across the fields again, far out to sea, something hooted, once, twice, and a third time wailing like a question.

A great dish of fire rose all of a sudden out of the sea and glared at Hob. He knew there was no one else it could see.

Chapter Thirteen

OWNSTAIRS, SALLY flung open a door. "A lovely morning," she said. "The sun is up and the air is clear. Wake up, children. Time for breakfast."

Hob stood where he was, on the roof beside the chimney. "Hob has been silly," he said to himself. "That is not a fire glaring at just me. It is the sun getting up in his usual place and looking at the whole world. Hob will forget his mistake and see whether there is breakfast for him, too."

He climbed down the roof, picked his way through the rose thorns, and went into the house.

The fire was alight. Hob found his place in the fender. To make certain someone knew he was here he rattled the poker and the tongs.

"It's Hob," said Katie. "We wanted him in the night."

"You had bad dreams," said Sally. "You are all right now, eating your breakfast. There is nothing the matter with you."

"Hob didn't help us," said Michael. "He doesn't deserve a cup of tea."

"What nonsense," said Sally. "But just in case,"

and she put a cup of tea beside the hearth and a slice of toast.

"I get lumps of coal," said the tongs. "Delicious."

"I get my nose warm," said the poker. "Great."

"I get a cup of tea," said Hob.

Breakfast went on around him. The children were made tidy and sent to school. Hob sat and thought. He got more tea when he rattled the cup and saucer.

"It's just the wind through the open door," Sally said. "It makes a noise like wanting more tea."

"She's a sensible girl," Hob told the poker. "But sense isn't what's required just now."

He wondered what was. Pyke had said that the way to set things right was to fetch the peddler. Before she had gone very far the pond had put out its tongue and the magpie had vanished.

"Gobbled up," said Hob.

"Bread dipped in bacon fat," said Sally, hearing him without knowing and handing down a tasty, greasy crust, "will float on those cups of tea, Hob."

Hob took the crust. He put it inside him, where it could float. It was magic to eat, warm and juicy, and it floated like anything.

"I shall have to look for Pyke," said Hob. "She is probably in the pond instead of on her urgent mission to the peddler. I shall get her out and send her on her way."

He knew what to do, but not how to do it. "Maybe there isn't a way," he thought. "I'll be up late. I should be in bed by now. But I must carry on."

He went out of the back door, into the farmyard. He crossed to the stable.

"Probably one somewhere," he said, looking for something, searching for what was needed. "Children often have them. If there was once a river, and there's still the sea. And the pond."

He searched the farm buildings. There was hay, there was straw, there were carts. There were machines. There were places cows had been. There was a sheepfold.

"Ducks would know," Hob said. "Ducky, Ducky," he called. There was no reply.

"Geese," said Hob, calling and calling "Goosey, Goosey." But there was no reply.

"Farmyard hens would not know what it was for," said Hob. "But they might have seen it."

There were no farmyard hens at all on this farm.

"I know that," said Hob. "There are no birds. So I shall go on looking."

"No," said the pig, when Hob asked. "Never seen anything like that. Scratch harder, please."

But Hob found what he was looking for, at the back of a barn, propped up and dry as dry. It was painted red and two oars were standing beside it.

Hob had no problem with the oars. He could carry those, one at a time. But the red boat they belonged to was far too solid for him.

"But I know who to ask," he said.

In the stable Mammoth and Mastodon were waiting to do their day's work.

"That thing is under your feet, Mammoth," said Mastodon. Hob was next to a great hoof with an iron shoe. "I can't see it but I can tell."

"Please keep still," said Hob. "I have to ask you something."

Mastodon put his broad head down and blew air from his nostrils at Hob. Mammoth bent his wide neck and puffed at him from the other side. Hob held a huge hairy leg, and managed to stay where he was.

He explained. He didn't explain exactly and fully because there was no need, and horses are more interested in their work than in the reasons for it. They thought what Hob wanted them to do was more like play, but they still did not want to know everything.

"We just do simple jobs," they said. "Plowing and harrowing and rolling and mowing and reaping and hauling and heaving. We don't know what it's for. At night we come into the stable to work at standing still until the next day. Where is the boat?"

Hob took them to it. "Tie a rope around my neck," said Mastodon. "Put it through that iron ring on the boat, then tie it around Mammoth's neck. You see, we know these things."

"He does," said Mammoth. "One day I shall know them, too."

"Ready?" said Mastodon. "Nice knots, Hob."

"Just ordinary," said Hob. "No Medicine Knots for now. Are you ready?"

"Tell us to pull," said Mastodon. "We do what

we're told. Get into the boat and have a ride."

Hob got in. "Start pulling," he said.

The horses started to pull.

"This doesn't feel like work," said Mastodon. "I couldn't do this day after day."

"Pulling feathers," said Mammoth. "Very tiring."

"Don't stop," said Hob, having a bumpy ride across the farmyard, down the track, over the field, and to the water's edge.

"We won't go in," said Mastodon. "It's not our kind of water."

"It's no one's water now," said Mammoth. "What's in there makes our manes stand on end."

They took the boat to the very edge. They said they would find their own way back to the stable. Hob thanked them. "If you have problems," he said, "send for me and I'll do what I can. Stones in your hooves or tangles in your tails."

He got to work and pushed and pulled the boat onto the water. He wondered all the time what the pond would do about it.

"I must get Pyke out," he said to himself. "She knows where the peddler is and when she finds him she will bring him back and we might be able to sort out all the problems. The children can get a good night's sleep, and I can get a day's rest."

He looked at the pond. The pond looked at him. The boat sat on the water. Water crept into the boat because all the planks had become dry and grown gaps. Then the water crept out again and ignored the boat.

"It won't be able to see me in there," thought
Hob. He climbed in. He had to stand on the seat
to use the oars and get them down to the water.

Hob pulled at the oars. The boat moved. "Quietly,"
said Hob. "So the pond doesn't notice."

Then he thought, "It isn't the pond, is it? It's
the thing in the pond. And I have no idea what
it is." But somewhere, he was sure, Pyke was
floating about.

"The pond doesn't like birds," he said. "Why?"

He got the boat to the middle, or a long way
from all the edges. He looked over the side.

"If she is under the water I shall be able to see
her," he said. "The water is so clear."

"And black as well," he thought.

He could see far through it, and then the
water stayed clear but got into a dark place.

"With twinkles," said Hob. "It has twinkles in
it. Why does it have that?"

He found a black and white thing floating and
picked it out with an oar. He spread it out and
looked at it.

It was a wing feather from a magpie.

"It is hers," he said. "She has fallen to pieces.
The rest of her is in the water. But she will not have
drowned. She is much too clever for that. If I can
find all of her then I can put her together and make
her work again. I must and I can and I will."

There was only one way to find her. Being in
the boat was not going to do the job.

Hob walked to the end of the seat and stood on the side of the boat.

"Should have brought some bubbles," he said, taking a deep breath.

Chapter Fourteen

T HE WATER WAS VERY COLD. Hob does not feel the cold if he does not want to. But you have to think of something before you can want it or not want it. Hob had not thought about this very cold water. His teeth began to ache.

"My tobacco will get wet," he said. A silvery bubble took the words away, like a puff of smoke with no flavor.

Hob saw his words pop out into the air. "It was warm up there," he said. "Next time Hob will count down from hot to cold, then zero, then . . ."

He did not finish what he was saying. All at once there was no light around him.

"I have counted down into darkness," he said. There was nothing above him, below him, to the sides, in front, or behind him.

Hob got used to it. "I can't change it," he said. "I'll look forward to something else."

He was looking forward to finding Pyke, so that she could bring the peddler back. He would know what to do about the Sea Serpent at sea, about storm and fright on land, and children curled up at the bottom of their beds.

The darkness grew darker, Hob thought. But black
is black and can't get blacker. "The dark is not darker,"
Hob said. He was quite full of water now and there
were no bubbles for the words. It was strange for
him to say them just in water.

"The dark is not darker," he repeated. "But the
dark is getting thicker, and nearly lumpy."

Hob was not falling through the pond anymore,
but walking on something solid.

It moved under his feet now and then, if he stood
still and thought about it. "Wobbling," he said. "It's
like being in sponge."

He thought about that. "Someone will come
and turn the sponge out and I shall be on top," he
decided. "If anyone fancies black sponge cake."

There was a little wobbling throb under his feet.

"Like a very far-off heart," Hob thought.

He began to walk about. "This sponge comes to
above my head on me," he said. "Also, it is not properly
mixed." He was finding hard bits like marbles in the
sponge, bright round things, glowing goldenish,
streaked with black spongeness. Hob wiped one
of them cleaner.

"I don't know what you are," he said. "Did you
fall off a Christmas Tree?"

The golden thing did not reply. It sat in Hob's
hands, giving off light.

"I think it's happy," said Hob. "And I can see
what I am doing."

It was alive, he thought, but not a talking thing.

"There are things that sit about giving light," he said. "But not in ponds."

But he began to wonder.

"No time for that," he said. "Not without a puff at the pipe, and a fireside. I have to look for Pyke, and now I have my lantern to do it with."

Hob looked around the whole pond. He spent all the time he needed. The bright thing showed him the way. He found two more feathers, and that was all.

"Three feathers do not make a magpie," he said. "What has become of her?"

He swam up to the boat. He could not lift the bright thing up. It was not heavy, but it was not coming up with him. He let it fall.

"It belongs to the dark," said Hob. "It won't come up out of it. I must get the dark out next."

He held onto the boat, reached down deep into the water, and got hold of the darkness itself.

"The peddler did this," he said. Hob was full of water and full of air, and his words were all foamy and strange, between a sneeze and a whistle.

He pulled on the darkness. He got an edge of it up to the surface.

He gathered a bundle of it under his arm, pulled at it, broke it off, and pushed it into the boat.

It sank into the bottom of the boat, limp and heavy.

"If I get it out," Hob said, because he knew he had to find the magpie, "I'll see the poor creature and dry her and send her on her way."

He collected another armful of darkness and

poured it into the boat. It settled into the bottom
and lay there like black water, almost fluffy on top.
There were one or two bright bits in it.

"No fish," said Hob, going down for more
blackness. "Nothing living in this pond, after all."

"Except Hob," he said, when he had breath for air.

Well, Hob is sometimes wrong.

Three more loads of darkness, and the boat was
getting full.

"I'll take it to the edge and dump it," thought Hob.
"Then come out here again and get the rest."

He climbed into the boat, stood on the thwart,
and rowed to the edge of the pond. He heaved all
the darkness out, and it lay in a heap on the bank.

"I need a cup of tea," he thought. "That I do."

You can't want something unless you think of it.
But the thing you want almost never comes just at
the right moment.

Yet Sally was walking down to the pond carrying
a cup of tea in one hand and a plate with a slice of
cake in the other.

"I'll just put it down here," she said. "My goodness,
who's playing with that old boat? I suppose George
let them, but I don't think it's a good idea. There, will
that do?" She put the saucer with its cup and the plate
with its cake on a flat stone and went away.

"It will do very nicely," said Hob. But Sally had
not been talking to him, he knew. She had been
looking around as she spoke, and never at Hob.

"But she spoke to me," said Hob. "It's mine."

He sat beside the tea and the cake.

"They're sitting beside me," he said. "They must have been waiting for me."

"Of course they are," said someone else. It was not Sally. She was nearly back at the house by now.

Pyke was perched in a tree, watching Hob.

"I don't know what you've been doing," she said. "I've been watching you and I can't understand it."

Hob nearly dropped his tea. He had several things to say to this tiresome bird.

"Why are you sitting in a tree?" he asked. "It's been hours since you set off. And why didn't you tell me you weren't in the pond? I've been looking for you all day. In fact it might be all week, it's so dark in there. Hurry to the peddler."

"I've been to the peddler," said Pyke. "Yes, I fell in the pond on the way. I climbed out, and had to walk the whole distance because I had lost so many feathers I could only fly in circles. I found the peddler, and he's on his way. I saw you when I got back, but no one knows what Hob does."

"Even Hob does not always know," said Hob. "He does his best. Did you walk back from the peddler?"

"I flew back," said Pyke. "That's how I get about. If you fly in circles you only get back to where you started from, so I could get back here. But I couldn't go where I wanted, unless I started from there. So here I am."

"I have wasted my time," said Hob. "But what's

time to Hob? He has more than anyone else.
And he is enjoying his cake more than ever."

"You could say thanks," said Pyke. "I got her
to bring it to you. I was flapped with a duster and
brushed with a broom before she understood."

Hob had to do something useful before stopping
his useless work. He picked up a shiny thing that had
fallen out of the darkness on the bank of the pond.
He wiped it until it was bright.

He knew what it was now. He had seen many
of them before. He dropped this one into the water.

"A star," he said. "I should have known. Night is
darkness, and darkness is night. In the pond the stars
are lumps in the night."

Then he was useful again. He carried his cup,
plate, and saucer back to the house.

"I shall wake you when he comes," said Pyke.

Hob yawned a good mouthful of Sleepy. "I'll be
in my cutch," he said.

"I think things will happen tonight," said Pyke.

"I'll be there," said Hob, which was what he
thought.

Chapter Fifteen

HOB WAS HALF WOKEN in broad daylight by the tinkling of little bells. He thought the magpie was teasing him, pretending that the peddler had come back in his cart with its little bells and red canvas roof.

"Stop it," he called. "I know what you do."

The little bells went on. Pyke would have stopped, and laughed, and thought her joke was over.

Hob could hear the children. They were shouting and happy, and slightly naughty, too, out in the road, with the peddler, cart, and donkey.

Hob woke right up. There might be danger in what was going on. He did not trust the peddler. Pyke was talking. He could not trust Pyke.

After all, between them they had sold him. Nobody had ever sold Hob before.

Nobody had ever bought Hob before. No one had sold Katie and Michael either.

"Children would not be useful," Hob said, climbing down from his cutch. "Or worth selling."

"What could you use them for?" he thought as he went across the kitchen.

"Could you eat them?" he wondered, getting

out into the garden. "With lots of sugar."

Michael and Katie were managing very well, not sold at all. They had heard little bells ringing while they were still in school, and caught up with the peddler on their way back. The peddler had been asleep, with the donkey doing all the work, plodding along, awake but surrounded by his galloping dreams.

The dreams had hidden themselves when Michael had run up behind the cart and climbed on. The peddler had not noticed. The donkey did not think there was extra weight, only that he was getting tired. That happened every day. He took no notice but went on carefully getting his feet in the right order.

"That one, this one, t'other one, the last one," he was repeating to himself. "How many have I got?"

Katie was running beside the cart, bowling one of the wheels along. She was running slowly because walking would have been too quick.

Michael had seen a strange hat sitting on a heap of clothes. The peddler was in the heap, fast asleep, not even dreaming.

Michael put the hat on, sat in the driver's place, and told the donkey to get a move on. "Gallop," he said. "Giddy up."

"I can't do it any quicker," the donkey was muttering. "And I'm sure I've got another leg somewhere."

"This is naughtiness," said Hob, at the garden gate, seeing the children at the cart down the road. "Or worse." Perhaps the peddler had not come at all, and only sent the cart.

Pyke came down from the roof of the house.

"He's in there," she said, when Hob said what he thought. "He's gathering his strength because we are going to need it."

"We must get the children away," said Hob. "They will annoy and upset him."

"He can turn them into mice," said Pyke. "They would like that."

Michael felt the hat being taken from his head. He saw the heap of rags stretch out a hand and take it. He saw the heap of rags sit up. He saw it smile at him. The peddler's smile was not a full and happy one. It was lopsided and wicked.

Michael jumped off the cart. He grabbed Katie's arm and pulled her away.

"They don't mean any harm," said Hob, getting there just at that time.

"I've known worse children," said the peddler. "Children that could do worse things if I let them."

"That's right," said Pyke.

Michael and Katie stayed to watch. They could see Hob, even in the sunshine. He had chosen to be seen so that no one could pretend he was not there.

"These two should go home," said Hob.

Michael and Katie voted not to go home.

"It might be bad," said Hob.

"It's sure to be," said Pyke.

"It was always going to be," said the peddler. "This is the time for it. This is the end of it."

"Good," said the donkey. "You legs, stop all this

'That one, this one, t'other one, the last one,' and stand still."

The cart stopped by the gate. The donkey went to sleep, dreams buzzing around his head like flies.

"Better look at the problem," said the peddler.

Hob knew the problem was at the pond, or in the pond, or under it. He led the way there.

Michael and Katie ran in front because they saw the boat on the water. They would have climbed in, but it was too far from the edge.

They saw the heap of blackness, the night that Hob had put on the shore. They went to look at that.

"That's a bad start," said the peddler. "Did you do this, Hob? It should be kept cold and dark, and you should have left it there."

"I spent all morning," said Hob. "I was looking for Pyke because I thought she might have drowned, but she had walked off to find you."

"Just looking for Pyke?" said the peddler. "You didn't find anything else?"

"Stars," said Hob. "And that heap of night over there."

"Those children are playing with it," said Pyke.

"It doesn't matter now," said the peddler. "Tell them to watch out for sharp stars, that's all. We've got something coming from the sea."

Michael and Katie thought the heap of night was black snow. They picked it up and threw it at each other. They began to build a black snowman, but they were not sure what to call it.

"It has served its purpose," said the peddler. "But I don't know how we are going to manage the rest. We shall have to do it very quickly, or there will be problems from the sea. I hear there have been storms. Have you any suggestions, Hob?"

"No," said Hob. "I can't get things right if I don't know what they are, and you've never told me. So I've done it wrong, and I haven't been any help here at all. You ought to give the money back and take me away."

The children did not like that idea. "We want to keep him," they called. "Hob, come and play in the black snow."

Hob was too busy. He had to find out what was going on, what had been going on all the time, what he had not been told.

"Does anybody know the problem?" he asked. "George, or Sally?"

"No," said the peddler. "I didn't want to frighten them. Silly people thought there might be treasure. I had better tell you, and we can figure out what to do."

"To save the house and the farm," said Pyke.

"And every field," said the peddler. "All that you can see. And we have to do it now."

"But," said Hob, "I am a house person only. I don't do landscapes."

"You're all we've got," said the peddler. "You and me. No one else knows enough to help us."

"I don't know what could happen to me," said Hob. "I've never died before, so that would be an experience. Is it as bad as that?"

"Worse," said the peddler. "If it goes wrong
then there's nowhere to be alive in."

"Tell him," said Pyke.

"Tell me," said Hob.

"We don't want the children to hear," said the
peddler. "Let's go across here. Then we shan't
frighten them out of their wits."

On the other side of the pond there was a quiet
place, stones to sit on, a wall to lean against, or perch
on if you were a magpie.

"They are scattering that night about," said the
peddler. "It's blowing everywhere on the breeze.
But it won't make any difference to us."

He was wrong.

"No," said Hob, agreeing with the peddler.

He was wrong.

"Not worth noticing," said Pyke.

She was wrong.

They were all wrong. A puff of wind took a sheaf
of night up into the air and dropped it over the wall
where Hob leaned and the magpie perched.

"I'll tell you all about the whole thing," said the
peddler. "I buy and sell land. All the land. I buy it from
the sea."

"Yes," said Hob, in darkness, in the cold of night.
He wondered where night was going.

"Home," said Night.

Pyke's teeth chattered. Or perhaps just her beak.
"Sudden bedtime," she said.

"Pretty cold," said the peddler. "Ugly cold. Here,

Hob, take this to keep you warm."

He pulled off his cloak, lifted off his hat, and put them both on Hob.

"I have been given clothes," said Hob. "I must leave. Where shall I go?"

"Home," said Night. "Home with us, into the kitchen of the night."

Hob went. He had been invited. The peddler went on talking in his darkness, but Hob did not hear.

———————— *Chapter Sixteen* ————————

"WAIT FOR US, HOB," someone shouted. "And for me, too," shouted another. "Children," said Hob. "I know children when I hear them. But I have forgotten already."

He had forgotten Michael and Katie. Their names had fallen out of his mind. He had left their house. He had been given something to wear, and gone away. He had been invited into another place, and that was where he was going, through the dark.

This time he had not put the clothes on. The cloak and the hat had been put on him.

"Not far to the house of Night," said the piece of night he was in. "Not far to home."

"It will be restful," thought Hob.

Michael and Katie were still calling and following far down below on the ground, in the fields.

"I've forgotten them, but I know their voices," said Hob.

The peddler was asking where Hob was. "Can Hob hear me?" he asked.

"Hob can hear you," said Hob, but not very loud. He belonged to another house now, and it would not be good manners to shout from there.

The night was rushing on and on. Hob was rushing with it.

"Is it far?" he asked. "Or is it like this all over?"

There was only dark around him. And back where it began, children calling his name.

"I can't help it," said Hob. "It's the rules."

"We need you," called Katie.

"Come back and help us," called Michael.

"Between us we can deal with it," called the peddler. "Before it is too late."

"Just a fly-by-night," shrieked Pyke, laughing in a tree, happy to see things go wrong.

Hob no longer heard. He had arrived at night.

"Out of breath," he said. "Head giving me Hat-Ache. Hob wouldn't mind a cup of tea. There's always tea in houses."

He looked around the place he had come to. There were stars to see by. On the earth below it was dark, because night is dark when you have to look through it. Up in it Hob could see.

"I'll just sit a moment and get my bearings," he said. "The stars are so clear it won't take long."

He was looking for North Star. It should have been in the north, but Hob could not find it. Hob guessed where north was in one bit of sky after another until he had looked everywhere. He still had not found North Star.

"I need that cup of tea," he thought. "My eyes aren't working their best. If it's Hat-Ache then the tea will help."

He rubbed his head, but the hat was still painful.
He rubbed his eyes, to make them see better.
"It hasn't done any good," he said a moment later.
His eyes were not looking for stars anymore, but
at the night all around him.
"Oh, dear," said Hob. "Dear me, and my goodness,
and here's a how-do-you-do."
He looked all around him again, to be sure.
"Someone has broken it," he said. "No wonder
I can't find North Star. No wonder sailors can't."
All around him was night.
Night was in a mess.
Night had been cracked.
Night had been pulled out of shape.
Night had holes in it.
Night had been smashed.
"It's been dropped," said Hob.
"Someone stole big pieces of me," said Night to
him. "And threw the rest about."
"Your furniture is upside down," said Hob. "Over
there is a fine, warm, summer night stuck in the middle
of December, and snow getting in. That's all wrong."
"The peddler," said Night. "The peddler took such
a lot of night away when he visited the end of the
world. He can't go there again – only once forever.
He took night away to wrap something in."
"Me," said Hob
"He wrapped up something different, long ago,"
said Night. "Wrapped it up to keep it cool and put
it in a pond."

"I heard something about that once," said Hob. "But it was a long time ago, or a great way off, and nothing to do with Hob."

"Of course not," said Night. "But all that the peddler took has come back now. But it does not know where it fits anymore because the rest of night has fallen to pieces."

Hob looked around him again. "I never saw such a mess," he said.

"Night has been wrecked," said Night. "I have been wrecked. We should go back to the end of the world and start again. You don't know what it is like, Hob, when Night does not feel at all well."

Night had a little cloudburst of tears, and felt very sorry for itself.

Hob felt very sorry for it, too. It had come rushing home only to find that everything had gone wrong.

"Nothing in the right place," said Night. "Nowhere in the right time. The stars have come loose, and the nights are in a daze."

And when Hob asked about it, there was no cup of tea either. Night could not find the teapot.

Overhead a star went out. Hob found a spare one, hoped it was the right size, and replaced it.

"Like changing a bulb," he said. "A daffodil instead of a tulip."

Hob began work without his tea, without his supper, without any help. He turned over the lost warm summer night, picked it up, gave it a shake to rid it of snow, found its cupboard, and put it away.

He shook December and stood it the right way
up on a wobbly bit of the night floor.

"What a dreadful mess," he said. "It's as matted as
knitting. You'd think a kitten had been playing in the
workbasket."

There was no kitten. But there was a Lion roaming
about, looking for its home.

"That's what men see when they look at the night,"
said Hob. "They think arrangements of stars look like
animals. But they don't say, 'Kitty, Kitty,' to it. Nor
does Hob."

Hob began to look about for other animals that
men put into the sky. When he saw them, "All out
of their cages," he said. "All hiding in the forest of
the night. All wild."

There was nothing for it but to get on with the
job. No tea, no supper, no cutch, and no rest.

"Because," said Hob, "when I have done this, then
I must go back to the peddler and the . . . what do they
call those little ones? Children, perhaps. I must go back
and deal with that."

Hob looked down through a cracked cloud and
saw the pond. It was spreading, getting bigger, the
water rising higher and beginning to run like a river
across the fields to the edge of the sea.

But up in the night the arrangements of stars had
gone wild.

Bull was happily stamping about, doing as he
liked. He put his head down and snorted at Hob.

"Groomph," he went, and scratched the ground

with his front hoof.

"I have to get you into your own field," said Hob. "Not wandering about the kitchen."

Bull put down a horn. He put it under Hob. Bull twitched. Hob went flying through the air.

"Keep thinking, Hob," said Hob.

"Hoomph," growled Bull, and went back to frightening other people of the night sky.

Chapter Seventeen

H OB LANDED IN SOME SOFT weather. He bounced, and was not hurt. Perhaps, though, Bull had not been the right place to start. Hob looked at other things.

Pieces of day were poking through. Edges had come unstitched.

"Night is no good at housekeeping," said Hob. "There are holes in it."

Hob pulled edges together. He darned holes. He tried to get the dark to stretch tight across the sky, without any leaky places. "It'll never end," he said. "But I have to do it. If a place wants sorting out, then it's my job."

"But at least," he told himself, "I was not sold to the sky, only stolen by it."

Someone was washing dishes. He could hear them swimming together and touching in the water.

"I am washing dishes until it is time to go to work," said Evening Star, doing housework. "I go out first each night to lead the rest. These days no one knows what time it is and no one gets up, so I don't set off, and everything is wrong."

"It is a complete muddle," said Hob.

"Be cross with them," said Evening Star.

"I can only do things one at a time," said Hob. "And the one I am cross with would always turn out to be in the right place already."

"I am having Sunset Tea," said Evening Star. "Would you care for a cup? If I read the tea leaves I'll know what kind of night it will be."

"Sunset Tea?" said Hob. "That will go down well."

Hob was sipping thoughtfully when Bull came roaring back through the night.

"Be careful, Hob," said Evening Star. "Bull breaks crockery and these are the last two cups."

Hob is not cross, or fierce. But it is his work to put things right, and things know that. Bull saw Hob standing where Bull wanted to run around.

"Grahoompheroomph," said Bull, waving his horns, thundering toward Hob, to move him.

Hob stood still. He stood firm. He stood so that he could not be moved. He can do that. He took a deep breath and stood in one place so that nothing else could ever be there. The tall and tattered hat stood so hard on him that his head ached like an iron thing.

Hob held up his hand. It was a sign for stopping. Bull saw that nothing would shift Hob. Bull knew who the headache was waiting for. Bull started to run backward as well as forward at the same time. There were sparks and stars under his hooves. There was the dust of stars around his head.

Hob hoped Hob would stand firm. "Stop," he said.

Bull stopped, with his horns on either side of Hob

and his Bull breath roaring in Hob's ears.

"This way," said Hob. "Where is your field? We are going to put you back in it." He laid a rope of stars on Bull and led him away.

When he came back from doing that, Evening Star had poured Hob more tea.

"But there are thousands more things in the wrong place," said Hob, looking at all the untidiness.

"Snake got out," said Evening Star. "So creepy and so crawly and so ill-tempered."

Hob went to look for Snake. He knew what to do for cross and crying worms. Snake was lost in an alarming night sky and in biting mood. Baby stars were twinkling with fright.

"I'll take your head," said Hob, soothingly.

"Nice," said Snake.

"And your tail," said Hob, sounding helpful.

"Oops," said Snake.

"And tie a Medicine Knot," said Hob. "That will help you not to be frightened or frightening." He crossed his hands over, pulled them apart, and there was Snake in a neat loop and feeling much better.

"Who's next?" said Hob.

North Star began to think he knew where he was, now that Bull and Snake were settled down. Starman with the Golden Belt began to tell his neighbors where to go. Fishy stars swam to the right place. Milky Way began to pour across the sky.

Hob was having to tell them to get into order. Many of them had no sense of their own. He had to rub some of them bright again.

"This is better," said Evening Star. "A set of good stars is better than tea leaves for telling a fortune. You are getting lucky, Hob."

"I am getting tired," said Hob.

"Something is following you," said Evening Star. "Calling your name."

Pyke was flying about calling for him. "Hob," she said, "come back and finish your job."

"I can't," said Hob. "Here I am wearing clothes and I can't take them off or come back."

"The thing in the pond is coming out," said Pyke. "It is waking up. The thing in the sea is coming out of the sea. You were meant to deal with both of them, Hob."

"Come back when I have sorted the stars," said Hob.

"There is no time," said Pyke. "It will be the end of everything. I shall be the last magpie and all the others will hate me." She left, very fluttery.

When he had time, Hob looked down. He saw the pond stretching. He saw the sea creeping nearer. He saw the waves beating and reaching out, and the land being washed away. He went back to tidying night.

"There's just as much to do now as there was at first," he said. "I wish I had some help."

Help came. There was one long black leg, and then another. There was a silver bubble, and another. Then more legs climbed up, and at the end of them the Great Water Spider and her luggage.

"Poor silly thing, Hob," she said, "coming up

here without any air. I've told you before, pack enough air and you can't go wrong."

Hob enjoys air, just as he enjoys tea, but he does not need it. It is no good telling a spider. She can't go without it or eat it raw.

"A few extra pairs of hands," she said. "Or feet. I work four times as fast as you, so let's get on with the job."

They got to work. The spider could stitch gaps up and hem night's edge and catch shooting stars, who were up to mischief as usual.

"And I always fancied a bite at that nice juicy moon, fat as a frog," she said, after a lot of work. "Are these stars all her spawn?"

"No," said Hob. "Spider, I think we've nearly finished. There are just those little rocky Asteroids to thread together."

"Then there will be Sunset Tea for you," said Evening Star. "And warm air for the Spider."

Hob went off on his last nightwork. The Asteroids are lumps of excitable rock, chasing each other and having rough fun at catch-as-catch-can. Hob was bumped and bruised and scratched.

"Got to keep moving," he said. "But they are so very rapid and hispid. Oh, dear, there goes my cloak. The peddler will never get it back now."

As he calmed the last Asteroid and tied the thread behind it, the first one caught up with him again. They go around and around kicking each other's heels.

"Forgot about that," said Hob.

He got out of the way. But the tall hat was nipped between two boulders, pulled away, bitten, sniffed at, carried along a bit, and then dropped.

It went crown over brim, turning and turning, smaller and smaller, right out of sight.

Somewhere far below it landed. Hob does not know where. There is a new mountain, waiting for a name. That was the peddler's hat. You can see it if you go that way, near Hatagonia.

"Now for a cup of tea," said Hob.

Evening Star was looking unhappily into her teapot. "I don't know where it came from," she said. "It wasn't there last time, and I hope it is not there next time. But at the moment it is disgusting."

In the teapot was SlyMe, snuggled against the spout, waiting for Hob.

"Hello, SlyYou," said Hob.

"You have strange friends," said Evening Star.

"I came out," said SlyMe. "Pond is coming up the pipe. Pond is spreading. Hob has to come home."

"I can't," said Hob. "I'm dressed for being here."

"Ah," said SlyMe. "Take a look at yourself."

Hob looked. There was just Hob there. The hispid Asteroids had torn up his cloak and whipped his hat from his head. Hob was ready to leave.

"Hob can go. He has stopped being here," he said.

"Come home," said SlyMe. "Stop the children from crying."

"Katie and Michael?" said Hob, remembering them. "They can stop their noise without me."

"Maybe," said SlyMe, "but there is another one. Come and deal with it."

"Another baby," said Hob. "Hob likes Baby."

"It might not be a baby," said SlyMe. "It might be full-grown. Come and rescue us."

Down below the children Hob knew were calling, "Star, star, star bright," and wishing for Hob.

"Very well," said Hob. "Hob's work is never done, and I'm still invited."

Chapter Eighteen

THE PEDDLER WAS ANGRY. "Where is my hat?" he shouted to Hob. His head was red and shiny and had wispy hair. "I keep all my words about buying and selling in my hat."

Hob had no idea where the hat was. He had fallen from the night sky into a heap of hay and just escaped being swallowed by Mastodon or Mammoth.

"Don't suppose you'll be any use," said Mastodon.

"They want help down at the pond," said Mammoth.

"All the fields we plowed have got water in them," said Mastodon.

"Don't call that good farming," said Mammoth.

"I'd better go and see," said Hob.

And when he had got there the peddler had been angry. He still was.

"You didn't hear anything I told you," said the peddler.

"No," said Hob. "So I don't know anything."

"Then I'd better tell you," said the peddler. "It's all my life's work in ruins, and the farm will be washed away. There will be nothing left."

Hob wondered what would become of him on

that day. Boggarts leave with the people if they can. But Hob has to be sent away with a new suit of clothes. It is the way to be rid of him. Then Hob goes away from the house. But if the house goes away from Hob that is different. What does Hob do?

The peddler did not care about that. "I thought you would sort that out when I sold you to George," he said.

Hob thought he had better go and look at the house at once, to see how things were. He thought the peddler should have been shouting at himself, not at Hob.

Things were as usual in the house. The fire was burning, there was tea on the table. There was space in the fender.

"Ah," said Sally, knowing Hob was there because the children had stopped quarreling. A cup of tea went down inside the fender, and a plate with a very large piece of cake on it.

"Real Tea," thought Hob. "Not Sunset Tea without sugar."

He warmed through by the fire. Tea made him feel like Hob again. Cake made him feel like two Hobs, except that there can only ever be one of him.

Sally was talking about the pond. It had been getting bigger and bigger. She talked about the sea. She said that it had been coming across the land through the fields.

"And something is swimming in it," said Michael.

"Shouting and shouting," said Katie. "Coming

nearer and nearer."

"It is time to get things sorted out," said Hob. "Keep the kettle hot, because I'll be back."

He left the kitchen. He left the house. He crossed the farmyard and went down to the pond again.

"Now what is it?" he said to the peddler. "What have you been doing?"

"I have been doing my best," said the peddler.

Pyke fell flat on her back and squawked to show that she was jeering at the peddler. "He hasn't got a best," she yelled. "Only a worst."

"I buy land from the sea," said the peddler. "That's where it gets made. Then I sell it to the farmers."

"Somewhere to put their fields," said Hob.

"Only magpies don't understand," said the peddler. "But the sea had a problem, a long time ago. There was a Sea Serpent. The Sea Serpent eats everything, the ships, the whales, the land, and it leaves salt sea instead."

Hob knew the Sea Serpent had been eating the land. "Go on," he said. "It does not sound like Hob's work, that is all."

"It was not peddler's work," said the peddler. "The Serpent was taking back the land I bought, and I thought it would take the whole country in the end. There would be nothing left, nowhere to walk, no houses, no fireside, no cooking, nothing to eat."

"Not even cake?" said Hob.

"Nothing," said the peddler. "And the farmers would want their money back from me."

"So what did he do, our wise peddler?" said Pyke.

"Tell them what you did."

"I shall have to say the word," said the peddler.

"Get it over with," said Pyke.

"If we have to do something we have to know what it is," said Hob.

"In the pond," said the peddler, "is the Sea Serpent's child. I took it from her and hid it there, and she does not know where it is. So she is hunting up and down the coast and biting off pieces of land until she finds it."

Hob did not approve of stealing the child. "It would miss its mother," he said. "That is unkind."

"Not at all," said the peddler. "It does not know anything about it."

"Of course it does," said Hob.

Pyke shook her head. The peddler shook his.

"It does not," he said. "The Sea Serpent's child is still an egg."

"Uh huh," said Pyke.

"Thump," went the ground. "Splash," went the pond, and a wave came rising out of it and washed over Hob's feet, up to his middle, onto his shoulders, and covered his head. Just in time he made himself unmovable, and took a deep breath.

In the house the smoke fell down the chimney. The teapot cracked. A window fell out. Katie ran to hide under the stairs, but Michael had got there first.

In the farm buildings Mammoth and Mastodon kicked at the stable door and let themselves out.

Pyke flew up into the air with a screech.

"And it is beginning to call for its mother," said the peddler. "If she comes there will be no land left between here and the sea for many miles."

"She is on her way," said Pyke from overhead. "Getting the stars right, which was not your job, was no help at all, Hob. She is using them to find her child. The land is being broken, the field gates are floating away."

"We brought the you-know-what, the oval thing, on a big ship," said the peddler. "We have to take it to the Sea Serpent before she gets here, or there will be only sea."

"How big is it?" said Hob. "An egg is not large." At once there was another heave in the pond, another wave, another window falling from the house.

"That big," said the peddler, catching Hob before he was washed away.

From the sea there was a huge shout. A chimney pot fell to the ground.

"It has a big child," said the peddler. "We need both the big horses to drag it from the pond. We need more than that to drag it to its mother."

"But children are children," said Hob. "I've met lots of them."

"One's enough," said the peddler. "That size. They lay them as big as a barn. How are we going to get it to the mother Sea Serpent without a big ship?"

"I don't know about that," said Hob. "Children are children. They can be taught to do things."

"But you can't train an . . . a roundish thing with a

shell," said the Peddler.

"Of course not," said Hob. "You can hard-boil them, and make an omelette, or a custard, but you can't train them."

"That's what I said," said the peddler. "So why don't you think of something? Here we are in the middle of the danger and you're supposed to be able to solve problems. What have you got in mind?"

"There are problems," said Hob, "that you haven't thought of. I can deal with them. But the problem you are telling me about isn't one at all. I can deal with that, too, because children are children. If you don't mind standing back, peddler, and keeping that bird in order, I will sort the matter out."

Hob rubbed his hands together and began to walk toward his task.

"If it doesn't work," he said to himself, "Hob won't have to worry about not having a house. I shan't be there to worry about anything."

Chapter Nineteen

"THIS POOR CHILD," said Hob, in the pond, ankle deep. "What a cruel thing you did, keeping it underwater, in the dark, no dreams, no mother to cluck-cluck-cluck to it."

"It didn't mind until the light got in," said the peddler. "It was happy until you unwrapped it."

"The mother minded," said Hob. "Now the child wants her. She can't get here because of all the land."

"We must get the egg . . ." said the peddler.

At the word Hob was washed out of the pond by a big wave, flat on his back. Pyke escaped with a few splashes. Away at the sea something shouted loud as earthquake, as strong as mountain, as wide as ocean.

". . . to the sea," the peddler went on.

"Nonsense," said Hob. "It's not just a shell with a thing inside. It's a thing with a shell outside. Now it wants to get out of the shell."

"Horses, big cart, it's huge," said the peddler.

Mammoth and Mastodon might be useful, but there was no need for a cart. Hob knew something simpler, though simple might not be safe. Hob had dreamed about the Sea Serpent and her long, sharp teeth. People dream fancies, but Hob dreams true. He knew about the tongue between the teeth, and the throat behind them. "I can be digested," he told himself, "by mother or baby."

"Get me a big silver spoon," he said. It was all he needed – silver spoon, kind heart, quick thinking, and good luck.

Michael brought the bright spoon, as long as Hob. Katie brought toast in case soldiers were needed.

Hob walked out into the pond with the spoon. With the night taken away he saw what he was walking on. It was eggshell. Very big eggshell, making the spoon look small.

"I will soon have you hatched," said Hob, "then you can walk yourself to mama." He tapped with the spoon. Something inside the eggshell tapped back.

"This child has an egg tooth," Hob said. The thing inside was too busy to notice the word. "Perhaps I am only a little one of my kind and can't remember what I am going to be. I shall be hatched with a wooden spoon, I suppose. Then where shall I go?"

What will hatch here? Hob wondered. What sort of child? Show me the child and I will tell you about its mother. I have seen the mother and . . .

He hit again with the spoon. The egg hit back, then Hob. They worked with tap and thud, tap and thud from both sides that Hob felt through his feet.

There was change. The noises became thump and bump, thump and bump. A crack began between Hob's feet. Another crossed it. The shell began to lift.

Hob stopped tapping. "You are just inside," he said.

"I don't want to hit you."

The egg tooth broke through the shell. The head of the Sea Serpent's child came up and looked around.

In its mouth each tooth was longer than Hob. For every one at the top there was another at the bottom. The mouth opened, and there was space between the rows of teeth.

"Where food goes," Hob said. "Baby is as big as the mother from up close. And probably hungry. I expected something that would be glad to see me."

The baby Sea Serpent was indeed glad to see Hob, not because he had hatched it, but because he was bite-sized and very near and not running away.

"I daren't move," Hob was thinking. "I've forgotten how. Oh, dear, and not a pretty child."

On the bank the peddler reached for his hat, but could not find it. Pyke flew farther away. Michael shouted for his father. George was in the yard harnessing the horses. Katie shouted at the baby serpent to leave Hob alone, you greedy thing.

Sally ran from the house with the frying pan in her hand. If there was a problem with the magpie she was going to swat that. She changed her mind and wanted to swat the baby serpent.

"No," called Hob. "Stay away. I can do this."

Baby serpent uncoiled out of its shell. It could not climb out. It was too long and heavy and the sharp edges hurt it. It snapped its teeth together.

Hob took hold of its head. He said, "Excuse me," reached down for its tail, and pulled a Medicine Knot into its middle. Now it felt happier.

"Only a wormlet," said Hob. "Or baby Snake."

Baby serpent took a deep breath and sniffed at Hob. Hob remembered the night sky, when Bull came charging down upon him and he had stood where he was. He turned immovable again, and would not shake or shift. Baby opened its mouth.

"I must be kind," Hob thought. "This child is hungry for food. Does it know Hob is not food?"

The child was more hungry for another thing. Hob was not its mother. It lifted its head and called for her, sad and seeking, lonely and longing.

Hob expected a reply from the sea. But there was none. The baby serpent expected one as well. Babies do. A great splash fell on Hob's head. The baby was weeping. Huge tears dropped from its eyes.

In the field Sally put her frying pan down. She understood. Katie burst into tears, too. She did not want Sally, but the mother Sea Serpent.

The Sea Serpent had been under the waves. Her child called again, and she replied at once.

The child heard. The child was pleased, and shouted back. The mother shouted, and the baby.

Clouds gathered overhead. Rain began to fall, lightning fluttered about, thunder limped loudly.

"Now listen," said Hob, bit by bit between shouts and shrieks and flashes and rumbles, "you'll have to walk down to the sea. We shall all help you, me, the children, their mother, the peddler, George with both horses."

"And the captain and crew," called a voice from overhead. The ship was coming down the lost river. Men threw the cargo overboard to keep them afloat.

They dropped ropes to Hob. He fastened them where he could on the slippery serpent child. The ship hoisted sails and began to pull.

The mother Sea Serpent was digging at the beach, tearing at the fields, making her way inland. Storm raged over her head. Wind sang in the hedges.

"Magpie," said Hob. "Tell the mother."

Pyke flew down to the sea and had lumps of cliff thrown at her until she gave Hob's message.

Hob was telling the serpent child what to tell its mother. It was so excited that it lost Hob among its teeth and nearly choked on him when he struggled against being swallowed.

"Moooommy," the creature shrieked.

"Baaaaby," called its mother, the great wind of its breath knocking the magpie out of the sky.

The long length of baby came out of the pond. It knocked the peddler over with its tail end.

"A big one," said Mastodon. "Lively."

"A baby," said Mammoth. "Sweet."

"All those things," said Hob, threading a rope among the tall teeth. "Pull, boys."

The donkey was in the road outside. "It's a mistake, all this fishing," he said. The long silvery side of the baby serpent crossed the road before his eyes. "But good weather for it."

Hob ran ahead. He expected the magpie to have

upset the mother Sea Serpent, but they were on the
beach, gossiping about raising eggs. Now and then
the serpent gave a honking call to the baby. The baby
was hurrying so much he had no breath to reply.

"He's on the way," said Hob.

"Time for us to go," said Pyke. She flew away.

The peddler followed. A little later the donkey-
cart trudged out of sight.

Peddler and cart, donkey and magpie, travel the sky
in search of the tall and patchwork hat. In his dreams
the donkey leaps the gate of stars.

"We didn't say Good-bye," said Sally.

"We should never have said Hello," said George.

Mother Sea Serpent and child Sea Serpent met
on the beach. They kissed and rattled their great teeth.
There were waterspouts and giant waves, hurrahs
and happinesses.

They went under the sea, out of sight. Waves and
storm slopped against the land for a time, and then
all was calm. The sun came out, the wind died down.
Far out to sea the ship of sailors sailed and sang.

"It is all over," said Hob.

"Best get back to work," said George. He lifted
Michael onto Mastodon and Katie onto Mammoth.

"Hob," said Katie. George said, "Nonsense," but
put Hob up in her lap. Sally sat behind, George rode
with Michael, and they went back to the farm.

A Giant Water Spider was arguing with a
duck about sharing the air, now they were living
in the pond.

Michael and Katie were picking up golden
money scattered on the grass, and feeling rich.

"Buttons," said George, looking at the coins.

In the kitchen there were sticky plates on the table.
"Slimy," said Sally.

"Good," said Hob. "He's back at work."

George raked up the kitchen fire. "A cup of tea
all around, I think," he said. "Boiled eggs."

Everybody stood still. Nothing bumped or shook.

"Perfect," said Hob. "Hob likes an egg."

"If it hasn't got Sea Serpent in it," says Hob.